A hallucinatory novel set deeply in the consciousness of a woman exploring a changed and frightening world.

Our protagonist comes to in a basement, tied to a chair, with a man looming over her. But someone has a knife.

We follow her as she emerges from captivity into an unnamed, nightmarish city, seeking some meaning to her new reality. As figures emerge from the night, some offering sanctuary, and others judgement, she keeps moving, making her way through this fever dream of a narrative. A haunting, embodied tale of alienation, fear, and the quest for respite.

Praise for

SUPPLICATION

"What an astonishing, indelible, and courageous book. I have never read anything like it. It entered my bloodstream. It takes every risk. *Supplication* is about the states of transformation women must endure and survive—every trial, loss, ascension, surrender, inhabitation is written so completely in its animal radiance, sensuality, and horror; the page can hardly hold the prose. The voice never breaks. Nour Abi-Nakhoul is a beautiful writer, conveying a hellscape, her sentences as direct as they are prismatic. So transforming, compulsive, and original."
—**Claudia Dey, author of** *Daughter*

"*Supplication* is as visceral and gripping as an actual nightmare, but also teeming with wisdom about selfhood and trauma and what it means to be alive. I couldn't put it down."
—**Ainslie Hogarth, author of** *Normal Women*

"Dreamy yet hard, propulsive yet ever-circling, Nour Abi-Nakhoul's *Supplication* reveals its mysteries slowly and painfully, as if withdrawing a dagger from its own viscera."
—**Davey Davis, author of** *X*

"Terrifying and poetic, *Supplication* twists the existentialism of Sartre's *Nausea* into a dark and disturbing form. Simultaneously cinematic horror and interior meditation, this book is as disorienting as Kafka at his most absurd. A philosophical reflection on the nature of selfhood and discontinuity that somehow manages to be both timeless and irresistibly urgent."
—Carrie Jenkins, author of *Sad Love*

"*Supplication* daringly explores a woman's enigmatic transfiguration after a terrifying traumatic event where surrender provided the only escape. It takes the reader on an incantatory pilgrimage through a surreal succession of nighttime wonders and horrors of an almost overwhelming intensity. As its mysteries unfold with quiet deliberation, *Supplication* seduces, repulses and mesmerizes. It painstakingly entwines the reader in an intricate web from which they will not want to escape."
—David Demchuk, author of *Red X*

"Full of foreboding and committed to depicting the extremes of interiority and the stinging incursions of the world into the self, *Supplication* evokes the work of Poe and Sadeq Hedayat while remaining alien and new."
—Naben Ruthnum, author of *The Grimmer*

SUPPLICATION

A Novel

Nour Abi-Nakhoul

STRANGE
LIGHT

Strange Light is a registered trademark of
Penguin Random House Canada Limited.

Library and Archives Canada Cataloguing in Publication

Title: Supplication : a novel / Nour Abi-Nakhoul.
Names: Abi-Nakhoul, Nour, author.

Identifiers: Canadiana (print) 20230482430 | Canadiana (ebook) 20230482449
| ISBN 9780771006074 (softcover) | ISBN 9780771006081 (EPUB)
Subjects: LCGFT: Novels.
Classification: LCC PS8601.B56 S87 2024 | DDC C813/.6—dc

This is a work of fiction. Names, characters, places, and incidents
either are the product of the author's imagination or are used
fictitiously. Any resemblance to actual persons, living or dead,
events, or locales is entirely coincidental.

Cover design: Emma Dolan
Cover art: Camilla Roder / Getty Images
Typeset by Terra Page
Printed in Canada

Published by Strange Light,
an imprint of Penguin Random House Canada Limited,
a Penguin Random House Company
www.penguinrandomhouse.ca

10 9 8 7 6 5 4 3 2 1

Penguin
Random House
Canada

SUPPLICATION

There was nothing before the moment of my eyes opening in the room. An instant held at arm's length from the conveyor belt of instants, suspended in its own little world, in a self-sufficient pod: a now without a before. Piercing the atmosphere of that moment's world was a direct plunge into the now; suddenly and without warning came the shock of the unending present, a raw and jagged edge. There, within the suddenness of the unending present, I was born— there I became *I*. That moment circled itself infinitely, spun on and on as though it would never end. To be born within that moment was to jump from a vertiginous height: the breathlessness of a body suspended, all quiet and hairs standing on end, skin cool in the whipping air. Then the chopping surface of the water below, ice-cold, ripping through the quietude, shredding everything that came before it: identity, history, memory, all torn wide open by the fall, the hole left behind gaping, delirious. The opening of my eyes in the damp dark room was my body smacking into the water, erasing everything that came before it, burning away the other possibilities of what I could have been. Birthing a new *I*, the *I* that was just a body hitting the water hard. Birthing the *I* that was just a body stuck there in the basement room, blood-shot eyes shooting open, panic coursing through veins instead of blood, as I grappled for the world. I became myself as a hook, scraping and tearing, wrestling with the new reality I found myself plunged into. Whatever came before the room, whatever was before the endless now, was torn to shreds. It was ripped apart by the scraping, tearing hook that was me opening my eyes.

When I opened my eyes it all flooded in at once, every detail clamouring for the attention of my pupils. My eyes were only open for a brief moment, but it was still enough for all of it to lunge into me, burning into my mind, stretching out the moment into infinity. I was frozen outside the passage of time, stuck in that singular moment looping around and around itself before my eyes, until I couldn't bear it any longer. If you're patient and allow it, a moment can expand or contract as much as it needs to, as much as the circumstances require. But if you try to resist the expanding and contracting of a moment's boundaries, try to push up against it and change it, something can break; you can lose your grip and dissipate beyond the boundaries of time, disintegrate into the gaps between the clock hand's stroke. This moment threw itself at me with such force, holding me hostage within it, slipping in through my eyes like a wild animal, that I squirmed desperately to get out of its grasp, unable to relax beneath its rabid insistence. My eyes snapped back shut, but the moment still whirred and knotted inside of me, its after-image burned onto the backs of my eyelids, its taste on my tongue, forcing me to see it, to know it.

What I saw within that moment were the miserable walls, interlocking grey stones whose cold I could feel viscerally in my fingers, as though I was putting my hand directly to them. Cracked and brittle, flecked by holes and erosion, the mortar in between them dry and flaking. Cold and miserable walls that housed hundreds and hundreds of timid bugs, their little mouths chewing and little legs scrabbling at the soft, worn-down parts of the mortar between the stones, burrowing holes and tunnels, racing with tiny, vibrating bodies through the elaborate labyrinth of their creation. Bugs that scattered swarmingly when the light moved toward them, scattered and squeezed themselves back into the shadows between the stones, their beady black eyes waiting and watching from the cool darkness. Everything in the room, everything that I saw in the moment I opened my eyes, was nothing but a stage for the insects to enact their drama: creeping and crawling, fighting and gorging, fucking and dying on the stage of the room. I didn't want to be the audience to their drama, that wasn't the part I wanted to play; I clenched my eyes tight to refuse it, but the drama still weaved itself through me, I could feel it pressing on me like the ominous gaze of a stranger on the back of your head. The problem was that the drama wasn't just the insects, crawling in their tunnels, fucking and dying, eating each other and shedding their exoskeletons; it was all of it. It was the walls the insects rubbed their dirty legs on, it was the floor beneath the walls where the exoskeletons and excretions would fall. The floor that was covered in dust, shadows, and darkness, and because of the darkness I couldn't tell what else there was, so anything else would have to be nameless.

But I did have a name for the two things standing on the floor faced toward me. Those boots with their wrinkled and cracked leather, the colour faded to a dirty brown, worn down with use and time. The boots stood on a part of the floor where the light was sparse, but despite the dark I could still see them: the crusty, hard laces, the scuffed-up toes. I didn't want to see them, but the vision of them snuck in when the rest of the moment thrust itself into me. I was unable to filter them out. And so I did have names for these things: the man's two feet in their boots. And names for other things, too, like the light bulb swinging overhead, casting its frail light downward onto the man's head. The light cast shadows down over the man's face, so that it was dark under the browbone, dark in the recesses which held the eyes, dark under the nose, dark under the cheekbones, dark beneath the chin. The rest of the face gathered the light, making it so I could see things I didn't want to in sharp detail, so I could instantly, easily recognize them, so that their names burst out of my mind effortlessly. Things that I didn't want to recognize, things that I didn't want to have names for, things that should have remained nameless: like the hair on top of the head, ungoverned and frantic, reaching out in all directions, and dark, nearly black, like what you see in a lightless room before your eyes adjust. Black hair the length of my smallest finger, sticking out in spikes and drooping down over the forehead, slick with sweat.

Beneath the hair the skin was pale, with pink and red rising up from underneath in certain places; on the cheeks, on the bridge of the nose, in between the eyebrows. There were creases in the skin, in the places where skin likes to jump and fold: across the forehead, underneath the eyes, around the mouth. In the places where the light didn't really touch—across the jawline, under the cheekbones, underneath the nose, inside the nostrils—hair rose up from under the skin and stood quivering against the world, dark and tiny, as thin and prickly as the hairs on an ant's leg. The eyes were set deep and dull into the pale pink face—into his pale pink face—tiny, buggy eyes, and inside them was a black as dark as the hair, black like the darkness of a lightless

room before your eyes adjust. The mouth—his mouth—
was slightly agape and drooling a little, ragged breath
going in and out, pulling the room into the body, into his
body, and pushing it back out. He and the room were
exactly the same; he was part of the dark floor, of the
cold grey walls, of the light bulb swinging slowly overhead. He held insects within his body, moving through
him swarmingly, burrowing and fucking and dying and
eating one another. But the man wasn't just the helpless
audience for the drama of the insects, he was an integral
part of it, and he could choose what part he wanted to
play. Not like me, who had not been given a way to choose,
who was confined to my role. Not like me, who was sitting tied to the chair in the damp basement room.

But it wasn't I that couldn't choose—it was whatever
came before *I*, it was that thing that had sat there helpless
and dull before everything began, before *I* opened my eyes
in this room. I didn't know for certain what that thing
preceding *I* was—everything before the current moment
had been set alight until it fell apart into ash, into dust.
There was no way to remember what I used to be without
projecting, fantasizing, like trying to conjure up memories that precede your birth. What I did know is that I had
become myself to have a way to choose, so that I wouldn't
just be wilted and anonymous in the chair, wrists bound
and breath held, desperately trying to disappear into a
crack in the floor while the room and the man and the

insects feverishly danced their drama around me. I
became myself to give myself a choice, gifting myself an
I, the kind of *I* that you could fill a room with, that you
could use to throw machines into motion. *I* is just a single syllable but there are so many directions in which it
can slide and crawl, slick, quiet, low to the ground and
watching. With it, I could tear feral claws into the space
before the present, leaving a tender wound. I could writhe
into the space after the inhale of the present moment,
I could fit myself coolly into the forward-crawl of time. I
didn't have to be the passive audience to the drama rolling around me, I could instead be a raw gash, impossible
to ignore, impossible to fit nicely into place; a gross
weeping sore in the room where the insects fucked and
shed their exoskeletons and the man stood smiling under
the light bulb's tragic swing.

I opened my eyes again, and there was the man's
shining delirious face, his hair matted with sweat and
hanging down over his brow, his crooked smile slanted
above his chin. Out of his mouth like a cough was *does
that hurt you child*, and the right answer was yes yes hor-
ribly yes, that's the part I was cast for. He slobbered like
a dog, one without loyalty or ties, unbound, tethered to
nothing except the raw animal impulse: the teeth, the
heaving breath, the hunger, the saliva glands. His breath
tore through him ragged and unstable, exhilarated by the
stage he had set, in frenzied excitement at the drama he

had taken control of. His spit dripping and puddling on the cold stone beneath us, thick and brown under the low light of the trembling bulb. *Child*, he called me, the word staining me red with grief. The grief throbbed and flowered, sizzling roughly, a grief that was expansive and demanding, that instead of folding in on itself asked for something different than what was. It asked for a route through which it could reimagine what was. I could route any path I liked; all the threads behind me had been undone with a single movement of my hand and there was nothing left to untether from. I wobbled in the freedom of the empty page, swung my head around looking for something to wind around my finger, a ring that I could be known by. *Child* was not a jewel that could adorn this grasp that had ripped and torn with its claws, I needed something else. But he was the owner of the drama that weaved through the room. I would be what he wanted me to be, but on my own terms. I would be a child, and like a child I would roll in the mud, unsightly and glorious, just like the dog he was: without ties, without constraint. I could only move within the scope of the drama itself; the man, the insects, the light bulb were there to keep the drama believing in itself, to prevent the intrusion of any lingering possibilities of *something else*, leaking saliva on the floor, tying me to the chair, casting shadows on the cold walls. I would have to break into a new possibility from within the scope of the drama that had been set—to chisel a ring for myself not from rare metals, not from rare stones, but from the grey rocks of the wall, from the light bulb's rusted chain.

And I could do it: I became myself, so I could become something else. So I could become the room, become the man, become the shadows and damp air, adopt the whole drama as my own. I could orient my desires, shape them into what I needed them to be. I reached inside myself, through the flesh and bone, and somewhere in there was the black pocket of my heart, and deep inside, so deep I had to really look for it, was an ability to want. I carefully slipped my fingers into it, and immediately the red grief inside me turned into fireworks, beautiful blooms of blue and white and gold. I slipped my fingers into this dark, faraway corner of my heart and stroked and caressed, coaxing out the kind of desire that could relax into the shape of my palm, willing and pliant and versatile. The kind of desire that could bend itself into whatever shape the circumstances demanded. A desire that could be trained and commanded like a good pet, lapping up whatever's in the open hand before it (whether it's milk or cyanide it still hits the tongue sweet). My desire wanted only and exactly what it needed to want, and wanted it so badly it couldn't keep still, trembling in place with dilating eyes. I wanted what I needed to want, wanted it so badly my breath fogged the air.

The man tightened the binds around my wrists and my desire pushed away, pushed up against the far edge of my heart, still too skittish, fleeing to hide in the corner. It still needed some coaching; I went over to it calmly, took it by the hand and whispered fortifying things into its ear, bringing it back into the open. The chair's hard arms pressed uncomfortably against the bones of my wrists, the dry rope cut into my skin, tense and burning, almost completely cutting my hands off from my still-pumping heart. With the tightness stinging my wrists I encouraged my desire to savour the sensation, to savour the painful stinging that electrified and stung my nerves. Encouraged my desire to anticipate the bruises that would rise up from under my skin, to adopt an attitude of curiosity and wonder; to be eager for what would come next. To be eager for the colours that would bob to the surface of my skin like fish rising from the depths of a lake to show the sun their shining faces, their gills sparkling with green and violet. My heart choked and throbbed as I led my desire out from its darkest corner, all the way out to the arms of the chair, letting it settle by the burning rope, by the wrists aching and bruised. And here, finally, the *yes* was drawn out of me, the *yes* spread through my whole body like the warmest rush. *Yes*, I desired this, *yes*, my desire had arrived, was here in the wrists that ached, in the skin that burned and split, in the bruises that rose to the surface and painted me with wonderful colours.

The *yes* was ready in my throat and in my heart, my heart that throbbed with want rather than with fear and grief.

Every aspect of the drama was still the same—the man controlled the room and I was bound to the chair before the swinging light bulb—but now any place before me would be the place where the sea meets the sand. My desire was the tide rolling itself over the landscape of tiny grains, licking hungrily at the gritty taste, with every movement pulling the coast into the water or pushing it away—locking it into a dance that annihilates their distinguished forms in preference of the ever-shifting meeting place between the two. My desire could transform everything with the foamy crash of its towering waves; the world wasn't anything but an arena in which my desire gave form to itself. My desire could shape the indistinct haze of the coast into a village of sandcastles, and I had grime and mud all over my hands and my face, my smiling face that was in love with the world I had created out of my want. The room was still the man's, the drama was still the same, but in the larger sense, in the only sense that mattered, I owned it all. Everything that greeted me could—would—become mine. I owned anything that I asked for, and I would shape it all in my image.

I let my desire emanate out from my body gently, giving it to the room carefully, like the gift that it was. I invited it to languorously stretch itself out, to touch the walls of the room, to graze the cold stones, to squeeze itself into the gaps between them. To wait comfortably in that quiet darkness until an insect cautiously approached with an antenna raised, and then to brush against those frail sensors. To rise up in the air and cradle the swinging light bulb, cradle that faint glow, to glide down to the ground and caress the crude wood of the chair I was bound to. My desire pressed itself against everything in the room until it could hold everything within itself, all of the bitter details. And then: *yes* I wanted the cold stone of the wall, *yes* I wanted the swarming crawl of the insects, *yes* I wanted the hard wood of the chair, *yes* I wanted the faded glow of the light bulb. I wanted it all, and once I wanted it, it was mine, the room was as much mine as it was the man's. As for him and his sweat-matted hair, his trembling jaw—I extended my desire's warm fingers to his rough skin, to the tiny coarse hairs that spotted his jawline. I reached into him with my desire to align myself with what he would do, to take his actions as my own, to reshape what he would give me into what I would take. Everything he would give to me would be what I would take from him, and he could do nothing to me other than what I would have done to me. I knew all of it, I took all of it into me, fit it into the expansiveness of my desire. And he knew it, felt my desire rooting around within him, the smile dripping off his face, the pink leaving his cheeks and nose, he faltered knowing that I had shifted my heart. That I had made it all mine, that it no longer mattered exactly what would be done—I wanted all of it, everything, it didn't matter what it was.

The blade was tucked into the man's frayed waistband, his thick fingers wrapped around its handle, slowly pulling it out. The blade was freckled by rust, dull and dirty, not sparkling in the dark like a death should. A death should glimmer like a star billions of miles away, dazzling and inexplicable and mysterious, and here my death was just a quotidian knife that had lain practical and unassuming on a tool bench for years. The man, eyes tiny and crazed, hair wet with sweat, showed me the knife from all its different angles, turning it around and around as I sat tied to the chair, his face glowing with some impenetrable happiness. And I wanted him to be showing me the knife, I wanted his eyes to dart delirious with their unnatural joy. What I wanted most was what was about to come, and the anticipation was gloriously unbearable. I knew it was about to come, just a few seconds longer, the knife turning around and around in the man's hand, and I was pining for it, panting with my heart stuck in my throat. A pang in my chest—I needed to have it then, it needed to be right then. I looked up at the man, his sweat-matted hair, his delirious eyes, his canine face, the insects swarming inside of him, and I let the *yes* leave me, let it pop right out of my mouth and into the room, and right as it left my lips the blade plunged into my side, just above the hip.

My whole self rushed to the place where the blade had hit me, till I wasn't anything other than the point where the sharpness met my body. I wasn't anything other than the wound, wasn't anything other than a place a knife could plunge into, a place where a knife slips in. And then I was also the place a knife pulls out of, the place where blood spurts oily and hot; but I wanted it to be so. The rusted blade, now red with my blood, plunged into me again—underneath my rib cage, near the heart that reached out with desire in lapping waves, that filled the room with it, that wrapped it around the handle of the blade, that wanted the blade to be plunging in. That wanted whatever happens, all of it, everything. The knife left me again, and then I was two wounds tied to the chair in the dark, damp room, a web of nerves screeching around them, electric and frenzied with the pain, with the rush of dizziness. As the blood fell out of me it took my eyes and ears with it, so that I couldn't feel the room around me anymore, couldn't feel the swinging light bulb, the insects swarming through the walls, the man standing in his worn boots. Everything was vanishing around me—just as I wanted it to be. All I was was the taste of brass, the loud shrill ringing swirling through my head, the shrieking red hue taking over me, and then even less than that as the ringing and red faded out of me, as they were replaced by only an overwhelming chill—just as I wanted it to be. And then it all stopped, even the feeling of cold, and it was over, over, everything over, all of it. Just as I wanted it to be. I took my death in my hands and left the room, cradling it like a delicate baby bird, floating up away from the room, from the man, from the whole drama. Leaving it behind.

It was the first time I died. When I finished dying I came back and the light bulb was still faintly lit, swinging gently over an empty room—no more blood soaking the floor, no more chair with harsh ropes wound around its arms, no more man standing there sweating and deliriously happy. He was somewhere else in the world, looking down at his hands, remembering the slickness of all the red that had come out of my body and soaked them. The breath rushed back into my body, ragged and frantic; with a start my heart jolted back into a tired, palpitating rhythm. The cold feeling evaporated out of me as I brightened back into life, my eyes and ears returning to me, the swirling in my head relaxing, steadying. I didn't want to be in the room anymore, the drama had run all the way to its end. The curtains must have been drawn without anyone telling me, my co-actor nowhere to be found. What I needed were flowers—the man should have left me with a beautiful bouquet in my arms, to mark the end of our production, the end of our dance atop the stage of the room. I moved unsteadily over to the door, placing my hand on the janky handle and leaning into it, shoving the heavy door outward with my hip. No one was there to see me leaving the stage except the insects, still burrowing in the mortar between the cold stones of the walls, watching and waiting from the dark, their feeble antennae twitching curiously.

Outside the door of the underground room was a dimly lit stairwell, all made of the same grey, cold stone as the basement, the steps chipped and cracked. The walls were rough and uneven like a natural rock formation, like the walls of a cave. The only light in the stairwell was emanating from a door at the top, radiating from the spaces at the bottom and the sides; I could see that the door had been left a little ajar, just by the tiniest crack. My feet slapped dully at the stone steps in their weathered and dirty shoes as the house creaked and buzzed around me: the chorus of old wood and electricity, whirring appliances and something else—a distant hum from deep within the stone walls, an implacable sound. I could hear it all from within the quiet of the basement stairway, murmurs coming from deep within the house, its whispered language, resonating out from a secret, unreachable place in between the stone walls, in between the stone steps. When I reached the top of the stairs the door slipped open readily at the brush of my weak hand, my trembling hand, and through the doorway light and new air fell onto my face like a dazzling sunrise. Breath moved in and out of me, expelling the damp darkness of the basement from my body, bringing in the fresh air. My eyes were so used to the dark they throbbed and squinted under the warm, orange-tinted glow of the upper-floor lights. My quick, darting eyes scanned the room frantically—I was an animal crouched in the woods, listening for the snap of a branch. But the house was empty. The man wasn't there, or if he was he'd somehow managed to shed his heavy plodding body. When I drank the clean air my tongue couldn't taste the canine sweat of his slobbering mouth, couldn't taste that stench of him, thick and fleshy like meat drying sweetly on a hook. I pierced the calm of the house with all of my senses, looking and listening and smelling the sighing walls that shifted and expanded and swayed, the air drifting through the space, yawning and placid, and there was nothing. No shuddering breath huddled in a dark corner, no floorboard bending ominously under the weight of a subtle footstep above my head. Though the lights were on, everything was quiet except the hiss and gasp of my breath pushing and pulling, and my heart, thumping through me with the quick kicks of a rabbit, fuzzy legs scraping my throat with every beat.

The house was like a furniture store after closing, like instead of climbing up from the basement I had entered by smashing a display window and crawling over the shards into a showroom. There were objects placed carefully throughout, but it was empty where it shouldn't have been, an obvious emptiness lurking beneath the facade of the furniture, something missing. It was like there hadn't ever been anyone there, like there never would be anyone there. If someone had lived there they must have done so without breathing or sweating or moving, they must have sat motionless in a chair, rotting quietly: greyed flesh falling off in chunks, limbs cracking into dust while the mailman knocked futilely at the door, the letterbox overflowing. Everything was in its right place, set up as a space to be lived in: walls, floor, ceiling, light fixtures, the long L of the couch, a matching armchair, sturdy ottoman at its foot, slim television affixed to the wall, photographs hanging in thin frames, an upper staircase with a tasteful rug running over its wooden steps, doors leading to other rooms, their silvery handles clean, shining. Through these doors there would inevitably be a place to cook, a place to eat, to sleep, to wash and use the toilet. But I couldn't believe in the existence of other rooms beyond the den I was in. Even if I had seen them I still wouldn't have believed in them. As I walked slowly through the den, running my fingers over the furniture, I still didn't believe the den was there, and in a way it wasn't.

The room was set up to make you believe there was a den there, every piece of furniture arranged as a *please* to the visitor, who should be convinced that they were standing in a place that existed in a way that mattered. The television on the wall, the sectional couch, everything was pleading with me to believe in it, but instead all that rose up inside me was anger, was defiance, because I wouldn't believe in it, not ever. It was all impossible: the stupidity of the matching furniture, the pretension of the well-placed pictures hanging on the wall, all the careful, delicate curation. Every time I blinked, my mind snagged on the thought that the den would be gone when my eyes opened again. But blinking didn't do anything to alter the scene, the room wouldn't shimmer away from me, it wanted my faith and would remain there, begging me, until I began believing in it or left. I would never believe in it, I couldn't bear to believe in it. I would turn away from it, avert my eyes, grab the handle of the front door and leave the house, before it hypnotized me.

Despite myself, I needed to see the extent of it. I stepped over to the wall closest to me and looked at one of the hanging pictures. The photograph was slightly grainy, with a warmth to it, the washed-out, nostalgic hues of an image printed before the break of the millennium. Because of this, the grass in the photo looked like it was starved for water, the sun and sky looked terribly bright, the whole landscape looked scorched with white heat. In the centre of the photograph were two figures, one of them bent down largely and awkwardly on his knee, the smaller one standing in front of him with a clumsy smile on her face, revealing a large gap in her teeth, cheap plastic sunglasses, a too-big bucket-shaped hat falling down almost over her eyes, hands hidden shyly behind her back. The man also had a slight smile on his face, a smile that looked like it was trying to contain itself for the camera, to stay restrained so he would look respectable and not silly. Still, the affection beneath the tiny smile couldn't be hidden: genuine happiness and love rose up through the man's face. This smile was nothing like the one he had given me down in the basement room. That smile hadn't beamed or shone or restrained itself politely; it had twitched and lunged and snarled as I sat before him tied to the chair, as I took my death from him. A smile without any happiness, only clammy exhilaration, nauseous excitement.

These two different smiles could never resonate with one another, could never make sense when lined up side by side. The distance between the two was disturbing me, was making all my muscles tremble and spasm. It was such a long way from one to the other—the gap was untraversable. There was no way for the smiles to inch together and close the gap, to look one another in the eye and clasp hands, acknowledge their brotherhood. In my mind I wrestled with them, tried to push them together, to line them up and make them greet one another. To sit with one another like matching dolls in a colourful plastic playhouse. I wanted them to sit there together, intimately, drinking tiny ceramic cups of make-believe fragrant tea, smiling and swapping stories, the borders around them evaporating as they became one. But they were planets away, wild wolves of no relation.

I dropped my eyes from the photograph on the wall. I couldn't look at any of the other ones, preserved perfectly in their neat frames, photos where the man was sure to be failing to conceal the joy of an affectionate smile, clasping hands with loved ones, posing in front of national monuments. I had to leave the house, break out from the nauseating gravitational pull of the perfect showroom den and go out onto the street—if there was anything out there on the street, if it wasn't all the same as this. I couldn't be shocked frozen and dizzy by another smile plastered on the man's face in a photo, another smile that I would have to try, and be unable, to reconcile: a smile that was bemused, polite, adoring, holding back a laugh. No, I couldn't hold those smiles in my heart, didn't have the strength to take them into my arms and close the gaps in between them, to set them up together like dolls and try to get them to play nice. They would crowd out the playhouse, cause a mutiny, overtake the order I was trying to impose: empty teacups smacking the ground, imaginary tea splashing everywhere, my bewildered eyes flicking between their faces, my heart throbbing painfully with the impossibility of crafting something out of the senselessness. The mutiny should have been mine, of course, not theirs, never theirs. Instead of trying to bring these smiles together I should burn the whole thing down. But no, I wouldn't be able to muster the energy to light the match. I didn't want the smiles in the first place, needed them all far, far away, to leave me enough space that I could stretch myself out and fall into a much-needed deep sleep.

Against the far wall of the den was a heavy door that connected the house with the world outside, a fragile portal to elsewhere. There was a stained-glass window on it, a tulip-shaped design dyed dark, the opaque petals barring you from looking through. The doorknob was golden, painted cheaply, the finish worn and faded. I wrapped my hand around the knob, tiny flakes of paint rubbing off into the creases of my skin, my palm's love and life lines filled with fool's gold. The knob wobbled in my hand as I began to slowly, carefully turn it, and while I turned it my head was filled with thoughts of the man and his daughter doing the same thing, hundreds and thousands of times, grasping the knob and turning it, tiny flakes of gold rubbing off into the skin of their hands, these flashing images of the man turning the knob injected forcibly into my mind, and when I looked at my hand it was the man's hand turning the doorknob. And I looked down at myself and I was the man, my torso the man's torso, my legs and feet the man's legs and feet, I was the man leaving the house at some point in the past, maybe yesterday, maybe a year ago, turning the doorknob in my large, clumsy hand. My hand was the man's hand turning the doorknob, and then suddenly my hand was the man's hand turning the knife into the space above my hip as I was tied to the chair. I looked up, and instead of the door I saw myself sitting there, losing blood and life, but on my face there wasn't pain or suffering or spite, only bliss and a fullness of love, the love of a saint starving to death of hunger, alone with her passions in the middle of the desert, transcendent and euphoric. But as I stared at my dying body tied to the chair something in those life-losing eyes shifted, and they were no longer filled with love but with snarling hate, saliva dripping from the mouth, eyes two black holes that would swallow, that would consume.

In shock I stepped away from the door and looked back down at my hand. There was no knife clasped in it. The hand was my own: my long scratching fingers, my raw knuckles, my dry, cracked skin. I grasped the knob again, turning it and pulling the door toward me, and my eyes pierced the dark of the world beyond, prying into what must have been night or very late evening. The sky was painted deep navy and wonderful, the sidewalks were

calm, clean and empty, and the road between the sidewalks was a dark, wide river, the whole scene docile and
at rest. I swept my head across the scene looking for
signs of movement, but there was nothing, not even an
insomniac bird or garbage-starved rat. The houses were
slumbering pigeons, nestled into themselves with their
eyes closed and their wings tucked. I watched the nighttime street from the doorway of the man's house like
I was a shock-still animal with giant eyes that sliced ner-
vously through the dark. Three steps down from the front
door of the house was a wide wood box, filled with dirt,
and there were bunches of flowers planted in it. Here was
the bouquet I was supposed to have, the one left for me
after the curtains were drawn on my final act. The street
was the backstage of the theatre, but there was no one
waiting there to see me, acknowledge me, congratulate
me, grasp my hand which longed to be grasped, my hand
which longed to be held and pulled along, pulled along
down the wide-river street, my hand which was filled to
bursting with *take me*, desiring not to be led to a specific
place but just to be taken. Longing so badly to be taken.
I had become myself to give myself a choice, but after
choosing my death I was tired, I didn't know where else
to go; I wanted to be led, to be guided.

But I had no hand to grasp, and so I wrapped my fingers around the stem of a flower, its petals a vivacious
orange, a thick, burning, shocking colour. The tiny petals

were layered in concentric circles, ripples that rolled out from the terrific earthquake that was the centre, the quaking centre that was a navel from which life and love flowed, from which life and love flowered outward, right into my hand that grasped it delicately, right into my eyes that bore witness to it, to the frenetic beauty of the flower. With a quick movement of my hand I yanked the flower so that it tore right at the bottom where the stem met the soil. In my hand the unremarkable violence of what I had done lay beautifully under the night sky: fragile velvety petals, the gradient of green across the stem, dark near the top and tender toward the frayed bottom edge, the terrible edge where I had shorn life from itself. I didn't continue to snap and tear at the flowers until I had a whole bouquet to myself. I wasn't greedy, one flower was enough, but a person should always have a flower to hold. If there isn't another hand in reach, a person should always have a flower to hold.

With the flower in my hand, courage came to me; a shy courage that was tethered to the stem for safekeeping, frail courage flowing back and forth between my hand and the flower's stem—and this flow between the two of us was a monument to not being alone. I wasn't alone, stranded and wraith-like in the midst of the dark street; I had life and love and beauty held tightly in my hand, close beside me. I had something, I was a person who had things, not like a shadow: a shadow can't grasp

anything, an incorporeal whisper flitting through the
night can't grasp anything at all, certainly not a beautiful flower, and yet here I was with a flower in my hand,
proving that I could exist in this world, and with this
proof came my bravery. I stepped further away from the
house and into the street, trying not to feel the house's
shape looming behind me, keeping away images of the
man outlined in the doorway, screeching and sweaty,
drenched in darkness. I put my foot carefully out against
the ground, then put my other foot in front of it, again
and again, and in this way I walked jerkily down the
street. The brutal street lamps towered above me, alien
tubes of concrete and hidden wire, each one with a huge
insect eye on its stretched neck, the eyes casting dim
egg-shaped circles of light against the dark concrete and
asphalt. As I walked I lunged into and emerged from
these eggs of light, birthed into the dark before once
again being swallowed by a circle of light, those glowing,
flickering wombs. The light admitted me and let me leave
every time without complaint, like soft hands pushing
gently on the small of my back, guiding me through the
dark, lonely night. Over and over I penetrated the egg
of light, the egg which is the impenetrable mystery of
pre-life, of death; I penetrated that impenetrable mystery as I walked, and I did so without pain or struggle.
And each time I left the egg I felt more ready to face the
terror of the lightless night, the terror of sombre reality;

my courage growing, the flower limp and beautiful in my hand, my breathing and pulse steady. The whole walk I didn't look anywhere but at the light cast by the street lamps: not over at the road, not at the quiet houses lined up beside the sidewalk, not at the blackness of the sky above. I didn't pay attention to anything else, I didn't let a thought bloom in my head, and before long I was standing outside the apartment building where I lived.

The soft hands within the eggs of light had pushed me all the way to the stage of my daily life: the facade of auburn bricks, the crooked plaque on which the building number could barely be read, the streaked, dirt-caked glass window on the front door. Concealed within this building were all of my habits, the motions of my everyday life, the life I had transcended and was now returning to. The keys for the building were in a purse I no longer had, that was buried within a previous life. I took the side of my fist and banged at the door, giving the building a heartbeat with my rhythm, *bang-bang, bang-bang, bang-bang*, a rhythm that was cut short—the heartbeat flatlining, the building sinking back into death—when the door swung open, revealing the landlord sleep-dazed and furious in a cheap nightdress. She was a squat woman with short, frizzy hair, a small, mean nose, a mouth that had been sketched too quickly. There, standing in the doorway in the middle of the night, her deep-set eyes were needles looking frantically for a vein in my neck, needles that hesitated just before they broke the skin, and instead drew back and traced me up and down, the poor ragged figure of me. *What happened to you*, she asked; I wasn't sure if something had happened or whether it was still happening, wasn't sure where to draw that line; and even if it had already happened, how could I say what it was—I could gesture vaguely, could shove ill-fitting, clunky blocks into some pathetic arrangement that would, at most, hint. I had nothing to give her, would never have anything to give someone who wanted to know what had happened to me, what was happening to me. They should know not to ask a question that couldn't be answered.

Instead, I told her something that she could understand: that I had lost my keys, that I had been mugged and my purse was stolen. She erupted at this, animated: *oh no, you know I'm always saying the city is so unsafe, you don't feel safe even walking down the street anymore, but really young women shouldn't be out alone, especially not at night, of course girls nowadays aren't as careful as they used to be, but let's take you upstairs,* her eyebrows raised and mouth set in such a way as to let me know she was only speaking half of her reproaches, that I was meant to guess at the rest—a piece of homework for me to take up to my apartment.

I stepped into the entryway, following her as she went up the flight of stairs continuing to speak, *I don't know what these people were thinking electing a mayor like that, he doesn't have any respect for the police, no respect for the law at all, it's no wonder this city's become a law-less place, practically a third-world country, animals running through the street doing whatever they want, if they'd built that new prison it wouldn't have become like this*, the creaky stairs with sad carpet running over them, faded by years of footsteps so you could barely see the original colours, all of it decayed into grey and brown, and within her torrent of words she kept glancing back with eyes that flicked over me, eyes that were thinking, cataloguing. When we reached the second floor there was a hallway of identical worn-down wooden doors, dirty shoes piled up alongside them on plastic racks. In front of the second door on the right the landlady fished a key from a large keyring and handed it to me, telling me that she would have to hire someone to change the locks, *since a criminal now has access to the building*, and that I was expected to cover the costs. I nodded and sent her away with a quick thanks, her thinking eyes slinking back down the hall, back to the cycles of habit that constituted her own life.

I fit the key into the lock and went into my apartment: the old wooden desk and mismatched plastic chair, the dark green walls lined with cracks and veins, the shelves with unpruned plants crowding over them, shrivelled and browned leaves wrestling with green ones for space. I turned left, where there were doorways to the bathroom and the bedroom perpendicular to one another. In the narrow bedroom the tiny mattress lay on the ground against the corner, covered by an old dark blue woollen throw; the nightstand next to it held a cheap plastic lamp and a disorganized stack of books, a light layer of dust covering all of it. I placed the flower carefully onto the books. Next to the bed I peeled my clothes off and stepped out of them, letting them stay crumpled where they fell, a chill brushing over my naked skin and bringing up goosebumps, the thin hairs on my arms and legs standing on end. I walked over to the bathroom, where a layer of grime that couldn't be scrubbed off coated the little white tiles on the wall. I knelt in front of the tub and twisted the knobs so that water flowed out—cold, cold, cold, then lukewarm, then warmer still. I plugged the drain, then waited on my knees for the bath to fill, arms and head resting on the edge of the tub, exhaustion wracking my body. When it was full I stopped the flow of the water and lifted my aching body over the edge of the tub and sank into the warmth; it took me in and cradled me lightly, I let the stillness surround me, I let the quiet seep into my pores, I lay unmoving with my eyes closed, my head tilted back. The drive that had brought me here left me; I didn't know what force could propel me into the future, with what tools I could create a future for myself.

Even like this, with my eyes closed and head tilted back, I noticed the thing's movements as soon as they began. I didn't need to see it to know it was there, wriggling serpentine out of the bath's faucet; I could just feel it, like you can feel the movements of your own limbs, and when I felt it moving a bolt of serenity ran through my body, my exhaustion leaving me. I flicked my eyes open because I wanted to watch it squirm: it looked like a braid of twisted hair, a gelatinous clump, thick and singular, commanding attention. It looked right back at me, looked at me without eyes, without a face, just featureless darkness. Shimmering against the environment, flickering like a glitch in the visual field of the room: dilating and contracting, growing thinner and then wider, shifting as though it didn't have any edges, any real boundaries that separated it from everything around it. The too-long length of it, endlessly falling out of the faucet, three feet long, four, five, squirming out of the tap and coiling its body in the water, twisting and turning in the bath above my body. Stretching itself out of the faucet, the mucous black of it, the dark fleshy rope. Twisting and moving through the water beside me, filling the bath with itself, water starting to slosh over the edge of the tub and spilling onto the dirty tiles. The thing brushed against my hip and it was like being touched by ice, jolting me with cold so that I gasped, the sensation vibrating through my spine, so cold it nearly hurt. It was soft, pliable, almost fleshy. It pushed against my hip until I got used to the cold, until the feeling didn't make me recoil, and then it moved up my body, pushing against my ribs, pressing against the flesh of my chest, intertwining with my long hair that floated in the water. It squirmed out of the faucet, so terribly long it seemed like it would never stop falling out, that it would continue to emerge until it filled up the whole tub, filled up the whole room, the whole apartment, the whole building—and then it was out. It was out of the faucet and all of it was in the water, twisting and serpentine, rearranging itself, inching away from my hips and ribs, retreating from my chest and my hair. It moved back and gathered its length, and I spread my legs in the water, looking at it, and without its face it looked back at me. Then it zipped quickly under the water and pushed inside me, all of it in an instant rushing into me, filling me up.

The pain, searing, screeching, burning, was a blessing, but at first I didn't recognize it as such. I flailed, grabbing desperately at the sides of the bathtub, frenzied, gasping and moaning, rolling my eyes around the room, searching for something to hold on to, something I could hold that would keep me tethered, so that I wouldn't disintegrate under the pain. Eyes racing over the sink, the tiled floor and walls, the bars of soap, the half-empty bottles of shampoo and conditioner, the cosmetics scattered around the sink. All of it flimsy, translucent, barely clinging to its own existence, none of it strong enough to hold me. None of it would hold me, I would shatter, shatter and scatter all across the tiled floor, but rising up before me within the inferno of pain was a question—would it be so bad to break? What was it that kept me scrabbling for something, that was desperate not to come apart under the weight of that unbearable pain? Here it was, this pain, placing itself so largely before me that I was forced to confront it—it was a blessing. It could be nothing other than a blessing, to bend and tear under the unflinching hand of a force far larger than myself; to through this tearing become a force far larger than myself, my body and mind screaming and singing with it, screaming and singing like I was saying a prayer, because I was. When I recognized the pain as a blessing, when I stopped seeking a barricade against it and instead welcomed it with open arms, it expanded and contorted, shifted itself into something else, something outside the dichotomy of pleasure and pain. The feeling warmed every part of me beatifically, from the chambers of my heart to the tiny bones in my feet. I relaxed and sank into it, and it stroked all of me with its electric animation, wonderful and horrible, adrenal and tender, both and neither, breaking me apart and fortifying me. I didn't care if it destroyed me—it would be glorious to be taken all the way to nothingness by that pain and terror which was a kind of love. But I wasn't taken all the way there, and instead as I lay in the bathtub the feeling gradually slipped away from me, the water cooling until it became tepid, and when it was tepid the feeling was gone. I rose carefully, my legs shaking, and stepped out of the bath. I pulled a white towel from the rod on the wall and wrapped it around my body, then moved over to the grimy mirror to look at myself.

In the reflection my lips were parted and wet, their pink hue coloured by the words held behind them, by the words I would bring out into the world, my language already nearly visible in the tiny beads of water on the lips. In the mirror I was bathed clean, my skin gleaming, still textured with goosebumps, collarbone pushing against the skin, the thin hair on my arms taut against the cool air. I opened my mouth to let go of my language, to give shape to the newfound prayer that coursed through all of me, that constituted every part of my body, that kept me tethered to the world, and to my prayer my lips quietly said only *yes, yes*. I towelled myself dry and dressed myself, and I went back out into the night.

When I walked into the bar, my eyes took a moment to adjust to the low light: it was a narrow space, with a long counter down the left side covered in stick-on veneer that made the particleboard look like dark wood. On the opposite side of the bar was a series of booths, stuffing oozing out of the ripped-up red vinyl of the seats. Toward the back, a mist of neon glow fumed upward from the slot machines that chirped and clinked over the room's conversations. My lips were coated with deep red, my eyes accentuated with sharp, black lines; a little leather purse, olive green, hung from my shoulder on a long strap—this is what the patrons in the bar saw as I walked in through the crooked door. The patrons who were throwing back their cloudy glasses, waterlogging their heads as they dangled their legs beneath the bar, whispering to each other in the booths over the rickety, shaking tables. Through the crooked door comes a woman, just a woman, with an olive green purse, with red-coloured lips, her eyes accentuated with sharp lines. This was what they saw, if they were close enough to notice these superficial details, if they decided to look up from their glasses, from the bar, from their conversational partner, as I took a few cautious steps into the dark room.

Under the low light of the bar I couldn't see anyone fishing into my eyes, but I knew there would be someone there, sitting in one of the darkened corners, peering at me, throwing lassoes or knives from across the room, grabbing me and placing me into their story. In any room I walked into there would always be someone taking me and placing me into their little playpen, gating me in, burying me alive as I sat there reading from the scripts they presented to me. If they did look up at me, squinted their eyes and focused, leaned closer to study me, maybe they saw things, or believed they saw things; immaterial things living hazy and amoebic under the mucous membranes of my eyes. They'd see whatever they wanted to see: things they desired, envied, quietly prayed for, wordlessly hated, silently fumed over. Anytime I walked into a room, any room, I couldn't breathe, the air always so heavy with other people's coercive imaginings; I could feel them piling up on my body, fur coat on fur coat, the heat and humidity thickening my lungs, my breath wheezing out thick and pained. It's impossible to walk into a room without someone blaming you for something, either happily or grudgingly; impossible to be yourself under the gaze of others, the gaze creating you as whatever antagonist or lover the looker needs, moulding you into that perfect porcelain object of affection, pity, resentment. Even a mirror is a room like this; when I'm in a mirror I fall under the watchful stranger's gaze of my own eyes, as I shape myself into whatever porcelain object I need to struggle or rest against. Even alone, there's no place away from the stranger's gaze.

I walked down the bar, past the placid bartender who lazily glanced up at me and then back down to the glass he was pouring a half-bottle of flat soda into. I swept my head left and right, looking for the person who I knew was looking at me. I'd almost walked through the whole place, the bottoms of my shoes sticking slightly to the dirty floor with each step, when I found them at a table in the corner, half-hidden behind the row of singing slot machines. They were sitting there with dark eyes like marbles sewed symmetrically into the fabric of their face, sparks of gold flaring in them and then fading as the lamp swung overhead, spraying its light intermittently like a disco ball. They were looking straight at me, seated politely and conscientiously with their back straight and hands clasped in their lap, their emotionless eyes glowing like headlights washing over me; but I was not the deer in the centre of the road, they were not the car speeding rashly toward me. They were like a cat balanced on a fence, looking at me through a window, motionless and calm as their glowing eyes dilated larger and larger, paws delicate on the tops of the posts. As I stood beside the table looking down at them they slowly pulled out a hand from the other one's grasp, uncurled its slender, manicured fingers and gestured for me to sit down. Nothing in their face moved, just the pulsing dark eyes trained on me, nearly all pupil and nothing inside them, all empty inside. I pulled out the chair across from them and sat, the hard, cheap material poking obnoxiously into my thighs and the tender space between my shoulders.

I studied them from across the table, the bar's mouldy, sweet-acidic smells suspended in the air between us. I couldn't tell if they were a man or a woman; their face was slender, with high cheekbones and a sharp nose, feminine or defined depending on the angle at which the light hit it. Dark wisps of hair fell over their forehead and around their ears and neck. Their eyes, massive and round, were ringed by a dark, purplish hue that spread out toward the bridge of their nose; fatigue, a bruise, or just a shadow crossing their face. They sat there looking back at me, like a reptile sunning itself in a sweltering garden; where was the long forked tongue that I knew was curled behind their teeth, that would snap out without warning? As I studied them I realized the whole room was a disorganized puzzle, the pieces spread haphazardly throughout it without reason or meaning; the bartender wiping down the counter, the machines calling out for coins, all of it insensible. It was this person's task to make something of it all: they were the measured hands clicking the jagged edges of everything into place.

Those beady eyes remained fixed on me, drinking in my limbs and hair, watching my skin as it breathed and sweat, saying nothing. I shifted in my uncomfortable seat; they were unmoving in theirs, their body just as speechless as their mouth, not giving me anything that would help me to gauge the situation, to help me place them in some way, to understand anything about them. The longer I looked at them the more opaque and uncertain their relationship to the world around them was, down to the most mundane aspects: I couldn't even see their breathing, couldn't say how the air moved in and out of their lungs; whether they took it in deeply or with hurried nervousness, whether they let it escape from their mouth or their nose. The more I studied them the less clear they were, like if I were to look for an hour they would cease to be recognizable as a person at all, would fade into their surroundings as something inanimate, immaterial, as if their existence in front of me was a kind of optical illusion, a trick my eyes were playing. Then, suddenly, they did move, their eyes leaving my face as they brought their hands up over the table and extended them toward me, holding a little rectangular box, slate black with a wide, frilly white ribbon tied into a bow around it. Overhead the lamp spun slightly and sprayed its light down at us, refracted through the red and yellow of the

stained glass, and underneath the light I was dizzy looking at the dark box, like the lamp was making me spin,
too. The person was holding the box out to me, their
giant marble eyes once more glued to my face, their long
fingers stretching over the edges of the box with nails
clean and pale like large curved teeth, which made the
hands mouths—but the mouths weren't eating, they were
gesturing for me to eat, to take the box and feast. I took
the box into my hands and it was heavier than I had
expected. The contrast between the white ribbon and the
dark box seemed sentimental, funereal, and the thought
that I was a widow accepting condolences rushed through
me, bringing tears to my eyes. I gently pulled at a tongue
of the ribbon until the bow came undone, and the ribbon
fell into my lap softly, a feather drifting from a bird.

I slid the lid off the box and looked inside, feeling as
though I had slit a fish from head to tail and was peering
into its body—like pulling apart the stitches of our world,
looking at an underside of things that I shouldn't be permitted entry into. Pulling back the curtain and revealing
the blood-soaked, twisted underbelly holding things up.
The interior of the box felt grossly private, vile. My stomach fluttered, flipping back and forth as I moved between
exhilaration and shame for having opened the box, but it
was too late to go back; the lid was off and I had already
looked. Inside was a scrunched bed of dark red tissue
paper, and lying on it was a pistol, black and clunky. It

looked vaguely unreal—in the way that all modern guns do, plasticky and toy-like, but also in the way that any weapon at all does when you first look at it. Weapons never look real to the eyes; it's only in the hand, when the heaviness of it presses against you directly, that the reality of it strikes you. I picked up the gun delicately and it was cool to the touch, textured on the handle that I was supposed to fold my fingers around, smooth at the front where the bullet would rush out, quick and brutal. I pushed a little button on the side and the magazine popped out the bottom; I pulled it out and looked inside, and there were the bullets stacked on top of each other, golden with rusty-orange tips. I pushed the magazine back into the gun, the click as it went into place shooting an electric thrill up my arm and into my chest which then spread through my whole body, making my nervous system flash wildly, giddy with excitement.

Discreetly, coolly, I slid the gun into my purse, where it would sit next to the big sunglasses, the plastic magnetized cards, the loose cash and receipt paper, all scattered carelessly in the bag, mixed together. I couldn't let go of any of the rubbish, couldn't organize the cards and cash neatly; the medley of it in there made me feel busy in a self-serious way, evidence of a life that was being lived wholly. Whenever I opened the bag the scene within showed me that every moment in my life was oriented toward the event that came next. The weapon added to that impression of satisfaction, of future-momentum, in a beautiful way. I snapped the purse closed and looked up from my lap; the person who had handed me the box was gone, dissipated into haze and smoke, into the air I was breathing. The space around their seat was slightly blurred, as though they'd been edited right out of the picture. I looked carefully at the blur, squinting, waiting for it to become more clear, but it wouldn't. After a couple minutes my eyes hurt, my temples throbbed deeply, nausea bloomed in my body. I gagged, feeling like I was going to vomit right in the middle of the bar, and averted my eyes from the blur, closing them and pressing on them with my thumbs so that I saw red.

I slung the purse's strap over my shoulder and stood up, the chair scraping noisily against the floor. I moved about the bar slowly, the bottoms of my shoes collecting dust and dirt, picking up the debris left behind by other footsteps, and all the debris was glowing bright with history, with the memories encoded within it. Every time I stepped I could feel the memories rising up through my shoes, up my legs to my mind, willing me to witness them. Walking past a table I stepped on a tiny cluster of soil, and couldn't keep myself from knowing that it had been brought into the bar by someone who had come straight from a public park; when I stepped on a fleck of toilet paper, that it had been tracked out from the bathroom by a woman who had been sitting in a stall with her ear pressed to her phone, listening to a long voicemail, a stream of agitated words coming out of the speaker as the side of the woman's face sweat, smearing the screen with perspiration; that when the voicemail ended she pressed a number on the screen to delete it and went out of the stall, out of the bathroom, out of the bar, her face very still, her mouth very tight. My feet kept picking up these things as I shuffled through the bar, and I didn't want to know; I just wanted to find the person who had given me the box. I felt the nausea stirring in me again, moving up from my chest into my throat, making the room shake and heave.

A man and woman were sitting next to each other in a booth, two tall glasses of straw-coloured beer perspiring onto the dirty table in front of them. They were tensed over the drinks they'd barely touched, slouched, with their shoulders hunched forward, speaking low and quiet to each other about something serious, their eyes stern and furtive, dancing around the room. The woman was spindly and taller than him, long arms flailing out of her thin frame, long blonde hair with darker roots peeking out, blush powdered on her cheeks and thick extensions glued to her eyelashes. His darker hair was cut short, nearly buzzed to the scalp, with stubble growing roughly out of his jawline and above his lips, a faded denim jacket around his shoulders. As I walked over I watched them stop whispering and reach for their glasses at the same time, taking little sips; the liquid slipping through them,

nudging open the creaky gates of their bodies. I stopped
by their table as they held their glasses up to their mouths,
their eyes flicking over to me, then they put the drinks
back on the table and turned their heads toward me expectantly, waiting for me to speak. In a careful voice I asked
them if they'd seen my friend, said I seemed to have mis-
placed them only a moment ago. Smiles flashed over their
mouths that didn't reach up into their eyes; the man asked
me what my friend looked like and I thought about it, trying and failing to find a way to describe them that would
be helpful. I said I wasn't too sure, and the woman let out
a thin, nervous laugh, the man smirking, his eyes glinting.
Must not be too important, then? he asked bemusedly, and
I slowly nodded, though I wasn't sure I agreed. The woman
smiled at me, gesturing to the other side of the booth,
sit with us instead!, the man nodding encouragingly. I slid
into the booth opposite them, sinking into the cushion
and placing my bag into my lap, conscious of the presence
of the gun inside, which I could see even through the fabric of the purse, with x-ray vision.

*Were you on a date, did he run out without paying the
bill?* the woman asked, a sharp, whimsical spark animating her face, leaning toward me with her elbows on the
table and hands under her chin. I sat quietly, my eyes
looking between them, not sure what to say, and the man
elbowed her softly, making her smile apologetically across
the table at me. There was fatigue in both their faces, grey

shadowing their eyes, creases around their mouths, a dull matte to their skin. I told them my friend had given something to me, but that I didn't know why, or who they were. The woman sat up straight and snapped her fingers animatedly, looking at me slyly. *A secret admirer!* she exclaimed, then leaned back against the booth, pleased, as though she had answered a lingering question. The man's phone dinged, and he looked down at it then over at the woman, who was looking at him expectantly, and he nodded subtly at her. He quickly picked up his glass and tipped it into his mouth, the knob on his throat moving up and down as he swallowed furiously, the liquid disappearing into his body. He placed the empty glass back on the table, half stood up and shuffled out of the booth. *Do you want a drink?* he asked me, and I shook my head no. The alcohol would have confused me, I needed to think carefully about what had happened, about whether anything had actually happened, whether there had been something that I had skipped over, that I had forgotten about. When I tried to think about it my thoughts slid back and forth, skidding over something that felt important; I would feel like I was getting close to the heart of the matter and then I would suddenly become lost in my mind, like there was a reel missing from the inside of my head; I needed to figure out how to replace it. I was sure there was something I was supposed to do to replace it, that would help me get to the core of what was happening.

With a shock I realized my face was wet, tears were falling slowly and evenly through my wide-open eyes as I remained silent and motionless, not bothering to wipe them. The woman faced me, not averting her gaze from the scene I was quietly making, and I blinked to unblur my vision and see her more clearly. In her eyes was fatigue, a tiredness that was so deep-rooted as to be materially tangible, wrapping itself around her irises and spreading through the whites of her eyes, dulling them, bringing up streaks of red veins. But there was warmth there, too, rising from somewhere behind her eyes. Somewhere behind her eyes she was there, back within the depths, watching and attempting to understand. I couldn't see exactly where she was in there, but I could see the diffuse movements, the scuffling as she tried to move forward to the surface of her eyes, tried to rise toward me. Through the dark of her pupils came a hand, two hands, pushing through the membranes and salt to offer themselves up to me, reaching toward me with their palms up, generous, meaning for me to move toward them and hold them with my own hands. I stiffened in my chair and looked quickly away from the woman, down at the dirty table, and my tears stopped flowing.

The man still hadn't returned; I looked over at the bar and he wasn't there, he must have gone out the front door; the bathroom was in the opposite direction. After a moment the woman asked me *what's the matter*, her face marred by confusion. The question struck at my throat, sharp and painful, making me tense and grow pale, grow paper-thin. Inside me somewhere a thing started to skid into being, to build itself up and up until it was mountainous, deafening, roaring and aflame; my heart pounding in time to the smoking engine of its core. My mouth dried up and I could feel the tension at the edges of my face, the discomfort where my body met the world, my eyes flitting around the room frantically, unable to decide what they were supposed to be focused on. I swallowed with difficulty and parted my dry lips to speak, the chapped skin sticking slightly; I told the woman that it was difficult for me to make sense of things, that they kept racing past me at such breakneck speed that I could barely make out the general shape of them, could barely understand the vague idea behind them, much less the details. That it was all too much to take in properly, that in the moment I could maybe grasp some part of them, but afterwards I was left with nothing, the scraps of the previous moment withering in my hands. That when I did try to revisit things I could see the colours and motions, but couldn't understand what any of it was supposed to mean; that I couldn't find my understanding, which was supposed to live under my skin, guiding my hand and eye, but wasn't there any longer. That every moment collapsed into itself as soon as it passed, and there was nothing left to hold on to; that all I had were my frail senses and faulty memory, and it

seemed there should be more than that. As I finished
speaking my eyes started to leak again, the tears blurring
the details of the dirty table's surface so that I couldn't
see the rings of perspiration or stains anymore.

The man suddenly reappeared, glancing over at me
and then at the woman, who communicated something
to him with her eyes that I couldn't pick up on. He nodded at her and she smiled slightly before swivelling her
head back to me. In the man's hands was another glass of
beer, which he slid in front of me before plopping down
in the booth. I wiped the tears from my eyes and looked
down at it, the tiny bubbles moving up to the surface of
the gold-tinged liquid, the sweet chemical smell drifting
up to me. I picked the glass up and tipped it so that the
drink, bitter and cold, trailed acidly down my throat,
feeling like it was eating at the flesh. I swallowed and the
coolness went down into my body, and tipped the glass
higher like the man had done, letting the liquid torrent
down inside me, gulping and gulping until I wasn't anything other than my mouth and throat, until there wasn't
anything other than the place where my body met the
liquid, the rest of me gone quiet, all my self concentrated
on that one point, endlessly drinking. With my mouth
gulping the beer I was drinking up the whole world, taking it into myself, my throat swallowing, the muscles of
my esophagus contracting around the liquid, pulling it
into me. The world beyond me could touch me, but only

in certain specific ways, and I didn't get to choose how the world could touch me. How awful, to not be able to choose the ways you can be touched by the world.

I placed the drained glass on the table, breathing heavily, some drops of sticky liquid dripping down my face. *Impressive*, the man laughed, leaning back in the booth with his arms crossed. The woman was smiling, but in her eyes was a glimmer of something else, careful, watching me. *What did you mean, there's nothing left to hold on to? I don't understand*, she said, scrunching her face at me, her eyes trained on my flushed cheeks, my face wet with beer and tears. I said that it was all insects bouncing off a car's windshield; they might leave a mark, residue, some blood, a section of a limb, but it didn't mean anything afterwards. I told her that I didn't know how I was supposed to understand the debris after the collision had passed, didn't know through which frame I was supposed to be looking at things. That I wanted something to hold on to that wouldn't melt away, something that would guide my eye, wrest open my vision, help me trace the trajectory that connected everything together. *Is that why you're crying*, the woman asked, and I didn't know, and I didn't think so, but I told her yes because that was who she wanted me to be, and I was willing to give her that, if it helped.

I wiped my wet face with the back of my hand and the two of them bent toward each other, speaking low so that

I couldn't hear them. After a quick exchange the woman leaned across the table close to me, speaking quietly, a kind smile on her face, her eyes dancing. *We're gonna go back to our apartment, do you wanna come with us?* My face stayed blank and uncomprehending, staring back at the woman until she continued: *we live right around the corner, we just picked up a little treat for us but we can share some with you, it seems like you're not having the best day.* Close to me, the woman's face was beautiful, her tiny nostrils moving slightly as she spoke, like a rabbit's curious nose. I slowly murmured in assent and she beamed back at me, looking at the man and nodding happily at him. The two of them slid out of the booth and stood, and I did the same, following them through the bar back to the front door, the woman glancing back at me to make sure I was behind them, flashing me an encouraging smile. I looked around, feeling the absence of the person who had given me the gun, which was heavy in my purse, swinging beside me slightly as I walked.

The room was littered with little lamps, crowding the floor, the desk, the nightstand, every available surface, like candles assembled for a mystic ceremony, dispersing a low warm glow. Novelty lights shaped like clowns, birds, soldiers, and cherubs; cheap spoofs of iconic mid-century fixtures, their paint chipped and colours fading; unremarkable plasticky items, their acrylic shades collecting dust. But all of them, despite their differences, emanated that same quality of light: soft, orange, friendly. There weren't any lights turned blazingly on overhead, scorching us with sharp white brashness, forcing us to see each other more clearly than we wanted to; to notice every pore and wrinkle, every eye's burst capillaries, the dryness of a knuckle or elbow. I wouldn't have been able to bear seeing the others clearly like that, these two strangers sitting on the floor across from me. If I caught sight of them or they caught sight of me illuminated in such cruel detail, it would have ruined what we were trying to do in that room: pretend to resonate with one another, convince each other of the facade of it. We weren't there to *truly* resonate, to laboriously climb into each other's hearts, hands sticky with dark blood, no; we all had our own reasons for coming together, quiet and private, private to each other and to ourselves as well. My own reasons lived inside my throat behind a flap of skin, hiding where I couldn't immediately reach without performing a grand excavation. I looked to the room around me, where the man and the woman lived: the shelves of knick-knacks on the walls—aged porcelain figures, glass animals, green glass bottles—the piles of debris on the desk and the floor, notebooks, letters, receipt paper, empty boxes; the plant in the corner, its leaves browning and withered. All these artifacts collaged into a portrait that was held up before my eyes, held in front of the reality of things, sparing me the horror of truly seeing. Giving me a way to know them without knowing them. To walk around without anything in front of your eyes, seeing things truthfully, staring directly into the blazing suns of others' faces, would be a nightmare, a punishment undeserved by even the most abject. I knew nothing of these strangers' hearts, and I wanted to know nothing of their hearts. It was better this way, for all of us; but we had to pretend that that wasn't so, to go through the motions.

Of course they didn't want to know anything of my heart, either, but what other choice did they have when presented with the spectre of it, the poor bruised heart of a poor bruised woman hovering skittishly in their field of vision like a phantom. If I had given them a proper glimpse, letting the cloak fall for a moment, we would have all recoiled in fear, shame, discomfort. The key is to give just enough that all parties are satisfied with the theatre of it, just enough that the illusion is sustained and everyone can continue to play their roles. If I gave nothing or if I gave too much, the whole thing would collapse and we'd be forced to go our separate ways. And I didn't want to go my separate way, I wanted to stay there suspended within the wonderful blooming that was taking place inside me, to stay within the warmth and softness that was wrapping itself around me, that was placing its quiet hands against my chest, my throat, my lungs, against my beating heart. Inside me was an unfolding, a process of transmutation that had begun after I'd sucked the orange powder into my nose. I had put my finger over the right side of my nose to close the nostril and leaned over the book when the man passed it to me, a hardcover copy of a murder mystery, its face marked with dozens of little indentations and scratches. I had put my nose to the powder neatly lined up on the book like an anteater eagerly touching its snout to the ground, hungrily breathing in a colony of ants. The pills weren't crushed up finely enough, so the larger chunks and flecks in the powder made me cough when they hit the back of my throat, chemical and slightly sweet, residue dripping out of my nostril down to

my lips, leaving an orange trail on the skin, staining it
with a gross artificial hue. When the powder fell down
into my body it turned into a rolling wind, expanding
me, pleasurably violent, spreading seeds through my
insides that quickly sprouted, the stalks growing upward
and outward, green foliage bursting out explosively—and
then came the flowers, the delicious fruit. I could taste their
overripe sweetness with my bones and my blood, their soft
bruised skins that would dribble with juice at just a light
touch, nearly rotten but not yet. The garden I had been
searching for, that we all spend our lives searching for, was
here within me. It was inside the confines of my own
body—I just hadn't known how to find it, how to tend to
it so it swelled, flowered, fragrant and sweet. Inside the
garden I shuddered, tiny shivering spasms, everything
pulsing, warm and tender. Finally, here was a thing I could
bear, glowing before me with a powerful brightness without burning my eyes or my skin. Finally, here was a thing
I could show reverence to; gracefully and with gratitude I
bowed before it, on my knees, lowering my head so my
forehead touched the ground. Bathed within the soft glow
I gave myself completely, thankfully. Suspended within
the pleasure of the garden, going limp before the pleasure
to let more of it enter me, surrendering so that the pleasure could be brought into ecstasy. To relinquish, to give
in, to give oneself completely to a thing outside of oneself,
to a thing shattering and absolute; yes. It was like what had

happened back in the bath, but stronger, more stable. Within that surrender was the utter joy of life, the joy of life at its smallest variable: the subtle, quotidian intricacies of the body and spirit, the immaterial, elusive wonder of being. I needed it, a thing to give myself over to, to humble myself before, to go limp in the face of; we all need it. There is nothing else.

Across from me the two strangers were lazily hunched over, the woman hugging her knees, the man with his legs splayed out in front of him and his back resting against the side of the bed. They were close to each other but not touching, their eyes downcast and half-closed, chatting slowly about something I wasn't making any effort to understand, just letting the words go past my ears as noise. They looked less held by the glow, not snug within it like I was, their journeys not ending in the garden, not able to remember the way there, if they had ever entered such a place to begin with. Their eyes flickered, dull, not finding a light bright enough to catch the pupil, to force it to constrict tenderly. They, like me, wanted something large enough to enclose the body and spirit within it, magnetic, looming and singular; their longing floated through the room like a stench, and I had to turn away from them so I wouldn't smell it. If it burrowed far enough into my nose it would find its way to the deeper recesses in my body, find a corner within me to claim, imprint itself upon the texture of my thoughts, over time stretching its reach

further and further, taking over more and more of me. I
didn't want to give any space within myself to them,
wouldn't let their feelings and sentimentalities flood into
me, encoding themselves within me, clawing and scraping,
changing me until I was unrecognizable. I wanted to know
nothing of their hearts, not really. I only wanted to remain
within the glow, within the garden, to concentrate on it.

I only wanted to remain suspended in that warmth, the
green and aromatic blooming, alive and vital. To remain
in that place where my insides were coated with moss,
dense and wild, the garden expanding through my whole
body; I willed the garden to stretch itself through my
body, giving myself up to it, letting it take control, letting
myself become overrun with it, become a vessel for it, fra-
grance and pollen and dirt flooding through my organs,
my limbs, my muscles and bones. My whole body becoming a garden, and deep inside, deep within the mossiest,
greenest, most untamed and fragrant centre of my body,
there was something else, looming there. Something that
wasn't flowers or foliage or dirt, sitting there half-hidden
in the middle of everything, camouflaging into the scenery,
twitching and dark against the chlorophyll-green grass.
I could've confused it for a shadow or a branch or a patch
of soil, unremarkable until I placed my full attention on it
and it suddenly became totally alien, suddenly became
something that didn't belong. Just like in the bath, it was a
long tube, glossy black like it was wet, its body convulsing

and twisting, the tail and head flicking frenetically. The head was smooth, tapered, featureless; no eyes, no mouth. Deep in the centre of my garden the eel-like thing turned its faceless head around and around, massive, slimy, and visceral, making my breath catch in my throat, sucking in all the air and light around it, impossible to ignore. It was looking for something, looking without eyes, sniffing for it in the damp, floral air, turning around and around. I was frozen, my attention fixed on it, this eel at the centre of my garden-body, half-hidden at the centre of the warm, pulsing glow that I had found within me. Turning its head around and around, twisting its slimy, thick body like an insect in the midst of a death rattle, its movements tinged with revolting, automatic desperation. It stopped and became still, its head suspended in the air, having sensed something, and I felt it see me, somehow I felt it see me. I felt it notice me as I floated omnisciently over my garden-body looking at it. A sick chill jolted through me, sharp and jagged with fear and unease, like the ground beneath me had just given way and made me plummet, my stomach up in my chest. It turned its head slowly toward me, looking directly at me with its featureless head, silent and calm, an animal about to pounce. I was unable to tear myself away, watching for what would come next. First there was just a sound, a damp clicking that reverberated out from the thing, a noise that I couldn't place. And then, quickly: the thing's black head split in two, split apart to reveal a mouth, rows and rows of teeth encircling the inside of its tube body, like some kind of ancient, bizarre weapon. The glossy, fleshy flaps of its head limply hung off it as it showed me its insides, as it showed me the sharp, thin, short teeth crammed into it, going back as far as I could see; as it showed me the garden that was inside its own body, violent and stark. It stayed facing me, mouth open, not lunging toward me, just wanting me to see, willing me to understand. It wanted me to sleep cradled in its razor mouth, with the rubbery, humid meat of its body wrapped all around me, with the teeth pushing up against me but not breaking my skin. It wanted me to trust its sharp mouth, to want to crawl inside and give my body up to it. It asked me to understand. I knew that if I understood I would crawl inside, that if I understood there would be no option other than to crawl inside; if I understood I would go limp before it and let myself be consumed by it. What was my garden, what were my foliage and flowers, to its teeth, to the brash, animal weapon of its body?

At that moment the flowers began to wilt. Their colours cycled from delicate pinks and vibrant oranges to grey, petals drooping and withering, the stems going brown and pale. The leaves fluttered off the trees, losing their moisture, disintegrating into tiny flakes. The green vanished from my garden-body, everything around the eel collapsing into ash, into dust. What was once a garden was suddenly dry and barren, a scorched place that would never again support life, a place where nothing could ever grow again. At the centre of the catastrophe the eel closed its mouth, the flaps of its head squelching back together to hide its teeth, and lowered itself to the ground, once again becoming unremarkable, blending into the brown, black, grey of the destroyed garden. Once again it was nothing peculiar, a shadow or a branch or a clump of dirt. I turned away from the garden at the centre of my body with a gasp, not able to bear it, the pain rushing through me like fire, throttling me, my head rolling, unable to see or breathe. I turned away from the ruins of the garden within me, the warm glow dissipating as I was thrust back out into the dead, numb world beyond it.

I clutched myself and bent over, sounds escaping from my mouth; underneath my skin was a lake of rolling pain, moving through my whole body, shrieking for attention. My eyes blurred so that I couldn't see anything, my head ringing out like a bell inside it had been struck. My pain was the pain of my devastated garden, the pain of the ashes and smoke floating up from it, filling me with heat and irritation. My grief weaved itself around me like a cord encircling my neck, tied my hands behind my back, left bruises all over my skin. There was nowhere for me to go, nothing for me to cling to.

The woman crossed the room, her hand light on my upper back, asking me something, her voice lilting with impersonal, rote concern and confusion. I could feel the clamminess of her hand through my shirt. The electric pain spread through me, the greyness and heat and grime; with effort I sat up straight, picking my head back up, folding my hands down and putting them into my lap as I crossed my legs. I smiled at the woman and waved her away, telling her I was fine. I didn't want to go through the dance, not in the state I was in, I didn't have the energy to play the game, to strike the perfect balance of expressing myself just enough, of obscuring myself just enough, to go back and forth with the woman there in that apartment. The man and the woman stared at me not unkindly, watching for something underneath the surface of my face's rippling expression. They wanted the pain to spring forth delicately, to be touched by my pain but not too hard, not too hot or too quick, just a light, fingertip-brush. They wanted to trace the outline of it, to briefly taste its bitterness on their tongues, and then to send it away. To meet it but not hold it. No one has the arms to hold it, yet their eyes flicker toward it, compulsive and curious. I couldn't go through with it, and maybe that was a blessing; I'd spare us all the dance, the morbid curiosity, the shame to follow.

I stared back at them, observing carefully as the man slipped another small handful of pills, tiny and orange, from a small plastic baggy and laid them out on the cover of the mystery novel. The woman watched him as he worked, her eyes following his movements as he took a plastic card and crushed the pills beneath it, rolling the hard bottom of his palm against the card, the pills crackling and popping as they were ground into dust. He took the card and with his finger brushed off the powder that was stuck to it, then took the edge of the card and sectioned the mess of powder into three long, straight lines. While he did this his mouth was moving subtly, language entering the air of the room, the woman picking it up and responding to it in turn, her mouth moving as well. I couldn't hear what they were saying, the ringing in my head blocking out everything else, their voices sounding as though we were separated by a thick wall. The man picked up a small piece of a straw and put one end in his nose, the other end pressed against the book, and in a swift motion sucked the largest line of powder into his head, leaning back and grimacing afterwards, his face scrunched up and eyes squinting as though in pain. He then picked up the book and the straw and carefully handed them over to the woman, who took them and repeated what he had done before handing the things over to me. I coughed when the powder hit my throat again, feeling the debris of the pills stuck in my head, feeling them drip down my body and splash into my bloodstream. The woman laughed at something the man said, then leaned back lazily against the side of the bed, the man's voice continuing low and fluid, looking between

me and her as he talked, though I hadn't been engaged
in the conversation since we'd entered the room, hadn't
processed a single word they'd said. I wasn't sure if they
had noticed and were being polite or if they hadn't realized at all. I didn't think I had any language left in me,
any route through which to relate to the environment
around me, which now sat at an uncrossable distance,
further and further away from me each moment. As I
looked at them, at the gloss of their skin, at the way
their mouths and bodies flailed and twitched as they
spoke, I was struck down by the improbability of it all.
The unlikeliness of me sitting there in that room, on
that night in particular, across from these two strangers,
was so massive that it couldn't be comprehended. It
wasn't only that, but everything else that went into this
moment: the existence of the room, of the two strangers, the fact of them living together, the fact of their
populating their apartment with that certain kind of
furniture, that certain kind of decor, those books, those
lamps. For each of these things to exist in their specific
iteration, to be arranged together in that room, alongside me and the strangers, out of an infinity of other
arrangements, an infinity of other ways things could be,
was incomprehensible, insensible, unbelievable. I couldn't
believe in it. We couldn't have been there, in that apartment together, the furniture and belongings strewn around
us. I wasn't there.

How could anything at all take place, under the weight of the sheer improbability that distributed its crushing pressure over everything? How could I be permitted to exist, to breathe, to move throughout the world, with the chances of anything so unfathomably low? The world should have been a void, a non-place where nothing ever happened, which gave shape to nothing. Maybe that is what it was, yet in our desperation, we were made to think it was not so, that the world was something other than a grand delusion. I began to tremble. A thought had presented itself to me, one that I was scared to think. The shape of it loomed darkly before me as I tried to avert my eyes from it. I knew I had touched something I wasn't supposed to, something that no one was supposed to touch; now, I knew the impossible, terrible truth of things. I had stumbled into a room hidden behind a false panel, where there lay something secret and obscure, the sight of which would irrevocably change the viewer. Inside my body the final ashes and detritus of the garden caved in, leaving an emptiness, a gaping hole in the middle of me. I felt I would soon flicker out of the world, fade into the floorboards leaving behind nothing, not even a memory. The two strangers wouldn't realize I had left, wouldn't remember taking me up to their apartment; my landlord wouldn't remember opening the building door for me, walking me up to my room. The whole night would be erased; my whole life erased. I looked at the strange man and woman and they were arguing light-heartedly about something, the woman rolling her eyes and smiling while the man's face shone with snarky amusement. I couldn't have them help me, couldn't have them understand; there was no way to cross the moat we had dug against mutual comprehension, and the room was getting further and further away from me, stretching itself out, the two of them tiny in the distance. I had lost every scrap of my understanding, of my ability to reach out and grasp something of the world that encircled me, and there was nowhere left to turn to. I felt a pang, a twisting pain over my hip, and remembered the knife entering me, back in the basement; remembered how the blood had left my body, pooling out on the concrete floor, and then how I had left my body, how I had died at his hands. I remembered this and I felt cold, I felt afraid.

And then, through the cold and the fear and confusion, there it was: what I had been waiting for all night. I hadn't known I was waiting for it until I heard it and knew that it was the answer to my questions, to my prayers. The sound cut through the room, crisp and clear. Relief washed over me, the ringing in my head and pain over my hip fleeing from me, the cold and fear vanishing. I recognized the sound immediately as the thing I had been anticipating. I scanned the room, trying to focus on it, find where it was sounding from, in insistent repetition, quick and tight, mechanical, industrial, *rap rap rap*

rap rap rap, the sounds just a second apart, unrelenting. It was quiet enough that it could be explained away as anything: an aspect of the plumbing or electricity, a shifting in the building, a trick of the ear, the oddly refracted echo of one's own heartbeat, but I knew what it was, knew that it wasn't something so benign, knew that it had entered the room explicitly to be understood by me. The other two didn't react at all, like they didn't hear it, because they couldn't understand; the significance of the sound wouldn't be revealed to them, but it revealed itself to me, naked and vulnerable, and I was grateful for that special position. I felt tenderness for the sound, felt warmth that heated the rabbit-thump of my heart.

Slowly I rose from the ground, my legs and feet feeling numb and unfamiliar, like my body belonged to someone else. I was unsteady and cautious as I hoisted myself up, stretching myself out, finding my balance against the apartment floor. The two of them looked over at me expectantly as I stood, their conversation trailing off as they waited for me to explain myself, faint smiles on their faces. I looked back at them blankly, taking in the creases in their skin, the dry, wispy hairs floating away from their heads, the tension in their bodies, all of it alien and incoherent. They looked at me and then around the room, quizzically, seeking what had roused me, what had changed me. Because everything in me was changed by the sound, everything was different. And it wasn't over yet—I was only beginning to approach an understanding of it, hadn't even come close to truly understanding. If they heard the sound, it passed over them without altering them, because it had nothing to do with them; they were inconsequential to this meeting between me and it, inconsequential to the entire night, which had formed specifically as a vessel to facilitate the meeting between me and the sound. All the while it continued to resound through the room and through my body, *rap rap rap rap rap rap*, shaking through me, opening me up, galvanizing me into activity. Hearing it, I was obliged to see it through, to move through the knocking into what would come afterwards.

Their eyes followed me as I moved past them, climbing onto the bed. It squeaked a bit under my weight, the springs bending, my feet sinking into the mattress. They scooched away from the bed, turned their bodies around while remaining seated so they could continue to watch me. Everything was quiet except for the sound and my careful movements toward it, the mattress groaning slightly under my feet as I moved toward the wall, my breath scraping through my mouth. The sound was booming and percussive, *rap rap rap rap rap rap*, louder now that I was closer to it, now that I was right beside it: it was a knocking resonating out from inside the wall. Standing on top of the bed I took my hand and placed the open palm against the wall; it was cool and roughly textured, the white paint thrown on in a bumpy, stippled way. With my hand on the wall the sound became physical, took over my body; it pounded in me like the throttling bass of a massive speaker, louder and more real than my heartbeat, shaking me, moving through me with a power that fuelled me, that took control of my bodily processes, giving my organs energy, transporting my blood, expanding and contracting my lungs. It was more than I could take, so immense that it hurt; pain jolted from my fingers up to my shoulder, my muscles straining under it. I gasped and let my hand drop off the wall, and as I did the knocking abruptly stopped. In its absence the depth of the silence was unbearable, shredding me apart so that I wanted to scream. It was gone before I sufficiently understood. I hadn't been able to bear it and it had fled from me. My eyes filled with tears, flooded with grief and shame. In the room was only my quiet weeping, my breath and pale heartbeat, the slight rustling of the strangers' bodies as they adjusted them. None of it was as real as the knocking had been. My arm and hand still vibrated with pain, but when I looked at my palm there was nothing there, not even any lingering redness. The knocking hadn't even left a memento I could use to remember it, a welt or burn that would prove that it had touched me.

It was just gone, as though it had never been there at all. Frantically I looked around the room, but it was all the same as it had been. The man and the woman were sitting there in silence staring at me, the smiles gone from their faces. I turned my gaze back to the wall, my eyes sprinting over its textured surface, putting my hands to it and running them over it, feeling the roughness scrape against the skin. I wanted to sink into the wall, to dissolve into it, for my body to be progressively shredded by the rough surface until there was nothing left of me in the room. My eyes glided over the wall, finding nothing, until I finally looked up, my head tilted back. Where the wall met the ceiling there was a thick black splotch, like wet paint suspended in a perpetually coagulated state rather than drying. It was the same texture, the same shade as the eel. The large blotch quivered and shimmered at the top of the wall like dark phlegm that had been hacked out of the raw, raspy throat of the building itself. I looked over to the strangers and they caught my eye with placid expressions, their eyes dull and lightless; they either didn't see the splotch or didn't realize its significance, the importance of this excretion that had been pushed out of the wall and into the room. It was for me to see, for me to understand. I looked back at it, watched it glisten and shine at the top of the wall. It started to move, bubbled and then began to drip down carefully, its form changing; abandoning itself in favour of what it would become. It streaked down the wall, liquid and thick, leaving a trail behind it, leaving parts of itself behind as it fell, getting smaller and smaller as it moved. I watched the streak on the wall get longer and longer as the dark splotch fell, and as it fell it communicated things to me, as it fell I began to understand. The further it dropped down the wall the more I understood, the understanding descending upon me slowly, in grades. As the splotch made its journey down the wall I was taking my own, synergistic, journey. By the time it went over the baseboard and touched the floor and its descent was over, it was miniscule, it had left its entire body as a streak on the wall. Through its movement it had become something else. And I too had become something else: I then finally understood, and my understanding lived inside me, altering me in myriad special ways. What I understood was that the knocking had stopped sounding out in the room not because it had fled from me and disappeared, but because it had provided itself to me. Through my open palm I had taken it into myself, it had dived into me and now we were entwined together complexly, inseparable. The knocking and I stood together on the bed in the apartment, surrounded by the lamps and books and tchotchkes, stared at by the two strangers seated on the floor. It was me and the knocking together, beaming and awash in understanding. We had transcended the meagre scope of what we were without the other, floated up to a higher plane where we loomed grandly, wrapped around each other like two snakes twisting into a tight embrace.

There was an interwovenness at play here that was greater than I, that made it so my movements weren't truly directed by me, my choices not really made by me. Through my meeting with the knocking the forces of the world beyond wormed through me, and I was so open to them: my skin so porous, my eyes wide open, my lips parted, the world rushing into me liquid, flooding me, quenching my thirst. I was flooded with the world, let it pour through me, drinking it up; I was the world itself, all of it existing within the confines of my body, my body just a mirror of the endlessness beyond it, my body only a way for the world to meet itself in every moment. My flesh forever jolting and spasming with all the jittering, swarming movements of the world. And all the white noise inside me, the quiet buzzing and humming that lurked there in the murky depths of my mind, was the chorus of the world, the voices of everything bundled together, overlapping each other, sighing and gasping and whispering and moaning, and if I paid attention I would see that all of it together became one voice and that the voice wanted to say something to me; to direct me, if only I would listen. That's what the knocking was, that's what the thing in the middle of the garden was. This was my blessing and my charge, my responsibility, and I needed to hoist it upon myself with all that I did, with every gesture of my hand, with every movement of my lips.

The voice would direct me if I listened, it would gently move my arm, move my foot, move my will, and all I had to do was fall to my knees before it and ask it to, give myself up to it and relax into its arms, let it carry me along. I only needed to give myself to it more absolutely. I could already hear it, could distantly hear the wet movements of its mouths as it spoke, its smacking lips and flicking tongues and gnashing teeth, could feel the shape of its whispers, the shape of its wants. This shape was dim, shrouded in fog, but it was easy to draw it closer, to bring it into clarity; the ability to do this came naturally to me, and I concentrated until, momentously, I could hear its voice more coherently than the sound of my own voice, loud and crisp and filling up my whole body, booming through me powerfully, and as soon as I could hear it in this way I understood completely, more completely than ever before. I understood what it was that I was doing, what I was meant to be doing, what my position was within this world. This understanding wrapped me up within itself, settling over me and materializing around my body like a nest, and as I peered out through this nest, everything was changed, irrevocably, and I understood everything, finally. With gratitude I understood everything.

The beating in my chest changed its tune, chirpy and strong rather than sluggish, wilted; the hues of the environment that encircled me shifted across the colour wheel, brightening, gaining depth, exploding into high-definition. Everything clicked and snapped into place rapidly, the scattered puzzle pieces revealing a picture that was confoundingly obvious. Of course that was how it was. But it was only once it snapped into place that I even realized it had been disjointed all that time, all that night, all my life. It was the clarity and meaningfulness that descends sweepingly onto a dreamscape once you're surprised to realize that you aren't awake. My body strengthened with the clarity, my breath moving in and out of me with surety and fullness. I was the stoic flat surface of an undisturbed pond once all the swimmers pack up and leave and the bullfrogs stop croaking, the clouds of gnats drift away, leaving the pond alone with nothing but its ponderous stillness. Everything superfluous fled out of me and I was left to meditate without interruption, and in a flash everything I was and needed to be rose up before me like a colossal mountain piercing through the cloudline overhead, the haze evaporating around it, the definition of its slopes and peaks sharpening.

When this clarity descended upon me it conferred to me that I carried something within my body that was ancient and fragile: the knocking on the wall, the creature in the bathtub, the black thing in the middle of the garden, all emanations of the same thing, different ways for a singular phenomenon to express itself. This thing was in the world but beyond it, had been here forever, longer than everything else, had spent millions of years standing on an elevated stoop and looking on as the world sprung up around it. But it was frail, easy to snap, easy to be subsumed within another thing and forgotten, to become banal. In order to remain sharp and magnificent it needed to keep itself apart, to remain obscure, evasive, and incomprehensible. It existed in an untraversable place beyond all else, in an unseen corner to the side of the world's stage, and its will was my will, and its will was the will of all things, the will of the world, and it lived inside me like a child; just like a child. It required reverence in equal part to protection, and it had chosen me to provide this for it, elected me as the thing that would cleave to its will and fulfill its desires, help it realize its purpose here in the world. And by realizing its purpose I would realize my own, my purpose to serve and protect it, to be its armour, its sword. This was my sacrament, my rite. The thing had emerged from behind its unpassable billowy curtain at the corner of the stage and entered me, and became a billion converging voices, their speech a language that preceded language; it became a coiled serpent, black and featureless and slimy. It became a child. Its mouths scratched and rubbed lovely against my insides, sending bizarre shivers across the scalp of my head, and I didn't need to listen to them with my ears, only to attune myself. Instinctively I knew what the child wanted, knew profoundly and intimately, could see clearly every contour of its will. I gave myself up with trust and grace, and I was made new.

I turned away from the wall and stepped gracefully off the bed, going to the others sitting on the floor. They watched me cautiously, their eyes half-closed, saying

nothing, the room quiet. There was something resonating from them, evaporating off of them and spreading
out into the air like perspiration. Something like anticipation lay there next to fear, breathless and eager.
Something had changed in them, just like I had changed,
my transmutation sending out ripples across the room
and touching everything around me. They were oriented
toward the future now, with all of their beings they
waited for what was to come rather than looking feebly
behind them and trying to hold on to things through
grief, guilt, lamentation. It was I who had given them
this, by changing before them and infecting them with
fear—fear and awe. By being the one with the child held
inside of me, by being the one who understood the journey that a black splotch makes as it slides down a wall, I
had enabled the man and the woman to look breathlessly
at what was to come. I was glad to have done this for them;
there, in that moment, there was nothing I wanted more
than to help them continue to anticipate breathlessly, to
help them look forever forward, to help them shake and
shiver and dilate their eyes against the horizon in the distance, sweating and panting and angling their chins at
what was to come. I was solemn as the weight of my new
responsibility settled over me, as I realized that with my
change came this burden of inducing changes in the others around me. After provoking these changes I couldn't
leave them like that, I needed to continue to sustain them,

to ensure that these changes didn't fade slowly from them and leave them the same as they were before, empty and disappointed. Within myself I sought generosity and grace, brought these aspects up toward the skin so that I radiated with them, so that they shone through me with fluorescent intensity. I had been gifted with such a singular blessing; it was only fair that I use it to offer something to the world, that I pay my dues and give back to the reality that had chosen me, that had helped me understand. This was what the child wanted.

I took a couple slow steps toward the woman. Her face was flushed slightly, a pattern of red moving over her cheeks and nose, breath moving in and out of her slightly open mouth, seated with her legs extended in front of her and her hands behind her against the floor. The room had become warm, I could feel the heat on the back of my neck. She looked up at me from the ground, expressionless, the fear and anticipation evaporating off of her, nearly visible, floating out from her mouth as she exhaled, floating up from her skin and hair as she perspired, I could almost see it in the air, I could almost reach out and touch it. Her eyes were blank, the pupils large and dark with nothing behind them, empty slates waiting for me to show them what was to come. I stepped forward again so I was directly above her, her head tipping back as she looked up at me, then I lowered myself so that I straddled her legs, sitting nearly in her lap. Her gaze was steady on me, those listless eyes that from up close I could see in detail. I could see clearly how dim and apathetic and unreacting they were. Then I blinked, and for a short, flickering moment that I nearly missed, that I could've missed if I wasn't paying attention, the eyes changed: for just a second they were shivering and crazed and wide with fear, and below them her mouth was moving, in the midst of saying something that I couldn't understand, before I blinked again and cut it off. Then the eyes were glazed over and lustreless once more, the face was flat, expressionless, the mouth unmoving. I blinked again and saw it again, saw her face animated and raving. It was like frames that had been spliced into a reel of film, that went by so quickly they nearly failed to make an impression on you. Where had they come from?

The misfitting frames flitted away, the scene stabilizing, the woman looking up at me with her eyes like two dark pits, lightless and unflickering. Like two dark pits watching, drawing me into them, into an endless fall without a bottom, a tunnel that went straight through the earth and beyond, into the dark emptiness of space. Looking into these eyes I felt a tingle at the top of my head, underneath the skin, that slid down the back of my neck, down my spine, spreading all the way to my tailbone and stopping there. Inside the eyes was silence that duplicated itself infinitely, hypnotic and alluring, and I was caught inside this multiplying silence, falling into it, the room around me blurring and going dark. My stomach dropped as I felt myself plummeting from a height, and then there was nothing, just black stretching in all directions forever; I couldn't even see where I had entered from, couldn't even see my own body, like my body had dematerialized, its matter claimed by the darkness. I had become a part of the darkness, too. I tried to move but couldn't feel anything, though there was no panic rising up within me, no feelings at all, just the limitless darkness and in the middle of it all the silent voice that was me. I relaxed into the darkness, and as I did it opened up just a crack; in front of me was a tear in the uniform black of the space, and from the tear pure white light shone out, sickly bright. Without being able to feel my body I twisted myself to move closer to the crack, wading toward it as though I was swimming, kicking and flailing with limbs I couldn't sense. I drifted toward it until I was just in front of it, and peered through the crack: inside everything was this unblemished matte white, the sameness destroying any sense of dimension so you couldn't tell where the space began or ended, whether there were any walls at all; but I could see there was a floor, because of the person sitting on it. His spindly, thin legs were crossed, his long dark hair falling down his shoulders and collecting in his lap. His eyes were closed, head angled downward. He murmured quietly to himself, something that I couldn't hear; I could just see his mouth moving, the dry, cracked lips opening and closing. Something was pouring out of him from the left side of his torso; a thick, black substance trickling from his body, collecting in a puddle on the matte white floor. I felt odd looking at the scene; I turned away from the white tear and back to the darkness, but began to go backward, to float back until I couldn't see the white tear at all anymore, and then the darkness collapsed around me, fizzled out until it was just the room in the strangers' apartment and I was staring at the woman's eyes.

The woman's eyes were weeping, tears dripping out the corners and down her cheeks. Surfacing out of the infinite black of the pupils, rising up and streaming translucent and salty down her face. I still couldn't feel my body; I felt that instead of hovering behind the surface of my eyes I was much further back, miles away from what I was seeing in the room. There was nothing I could touch—I reached out and touched the woman's face and it was like only my hand touched her, not me; only the flesh and bone and skin, but not me. She didn't move as my fingertips pressed lightly against her cheek and then withdrew. Beside us the man was still sitting, watching us with the same expression as the woman: dull and unengaged, his eyelids heavy over his eyes with their large black pupils, waiting for me to show them what was to come. This wasn't what I wanted, none of this was what I wanted, but I needed to have faith, to lean in and let myself be guided by the splotch of black ink that had dripped down the wall, let myself be guided by the knocking as it

resonated from within my heart, let myself be guided by
the eel with its razor mouth. I needed to give myself up
to the child and trust it to pave a path for me, to let me
know where I was supposed to go. If I gave myself up to
it I could let the blessing I had received expand out into
the world, I could let it touch everything around me, let it
bless those around me as well. In the room I closed my
eyes and let myself be pulled toward the reality that I
would create, the reality that I would give shape to. I had
given the man and the woman the gift of breathless anticipation, and they were waiting eagerly to see what came
next, and to sit there waiting was a blessing—but there
couldn't be breathless anticipation without what would
come after.

What followed needed form, sharp, discrete, strong,
and beautiful. This would be my second gift: everything I
had done had moved me toward this point, everything
would be brought to its zenith when what I needed to do
was done. I floated forward into the reality that I was creating, let myself be pulled along by its hefty gravitational
pull, shaved away the last parts of me that resisted it, that
protested against it. I stood up and stepped away from the
woman, going back over to the other side of the room,
away from the bed. They both watched me as I moved,
with the same lightless depth in their eyes, mirror images
of each other. As I moved they shifted their bodies over
slowly so they could keep looking at me. I knelt on the

floor, picking up my bag, opening the clasp. I reached in
and took out the handgun, and it fit into my hands like it
was a part of them, like it had grown tumorous out of
the flesh and then callused, turned hard and dangerous.
The knocking in my chest grew louder, all-encompassing,
boomed through my body, filling the room, *rap rap rap
rap rap rap*. I looked down at the gun and it was as though
the room was wrapping itself around it, like reality was
bending around the tiny machine, cradling it, synchro-
nizing with it. The room contracted itself around the gun
and the metal was cool against my hands, and everything
was waiting for what was to come: the man and the
woman and me and the apartment as well, and the whole
night as well. They looked over at me with their lightless
eyes and didn't move, anticipating what was going to happen, waiting for what would come, and there was nothing
for me to do except give it to them: I pointed the gun and
my finger wrapped around the trigger and the room
pulsed against the gun, and the knocking inside me was
deafeningly loud, and the man and the woman still stared
at me, waiting for what would come. I twitched against
the trigger and the man moved, bounding up from the
floor and swinging his body toward me, like the room
was pushing him toward me, was pushing the both of us
toward what would come. I closed my eyes and without
thinking did what I was meant to do: the sound of the
shot was explosive and final, the machine jerking back in

my hand so that I almost lost my grip on it. A pungent smell floated up from the gun, sharp and smoky and chemical, and I opened my eyes to look at him. He was lying on the floor, his body shorn apart, blood and bone and spasms, hot liquid gurgling out of his mouth. This was what came after the waiting, this was what he had been anticipating, what he had called toward him, what I had given him. This was the answer, the shape of the blessing, what the black splotch had intimated as it dripped down the wall. The woman seated beside him hadn't moved, was still watching me quietly, the endlessness of her black eyes turned to me, calmly waiting. The blood of the man's body flowed toward her. Now she had seen what would come after, and all she had to do was wait for it to approach her, to wrap itself around her. I cocked back the hammer of the gun and turned it to her, let the knocking rise up in me, let it rise up and fill my body, whipping through me, expanding from my chest out into my limbs, down my arms, down to the hands that held the gun, let it guide my fingers as they moved against the machine. Then, sudden and final, the explosive bark, the fire and swiftness, as I pulled the trigger and the bullet flew across the room and injected itself into the body of the woman. Her body twisted and then flopped to the floor, beside the man, the growing pools of their blood intersecting, painting the room in maroons and crimsons, and then they weren't themselves anymore, then there were two lifeless things on the floor and it was done. I had done what I needed to do.

The knocking sped up within me into an allegro, *rap rap rap rap rap rap,* and then slowed till it stopped, and then the room was quiet. There was nothing left except my breath, moving raggedly out of my open mouth. The weapon was dull and tired in my hand, suddenly heavy; the feeling was back in my body, fatigue and tension running through all the taut ropes of my muscles. And I was flattened by the vertigo, by the way the room spun, by how everything was disoriented by the presence of all the blood pooling on the floor. Inside me, hidden deep inside, the part of me that watches was awash in all of it, the blood and the bodies, the way the apartment had inverted, the conclusion of the blessing; it was bathed in all of it, everything. It couldn't look away.

I left the two of them on the floor with the crimson rippling out of their bodies, holes in their bodies through which the hot metal had ripped, quick and powerful and fiery. I slipped my shoes on and went out the door, closing it carefully behind me, then down the stale hallway, down the ugly concrete stairs, out of the building and into the street. I turned and looked up at the strangers' apartment window and it was glowing against the night air with the orange light from all the little lamps, the curtains open. I stood there in the street looking up at the window, watching, waiting for something to happen, for the strange woman or man to approach and look down, back at me, but there was only the empty window. The two of them wouldn't approach the window, wouldn't come down to the street, because of what I had done to them. And what I had done was share my blessing with them, was let generosity emanate from my pores. I had been saint-like, the blessing glowing out of me like bioluminescence, brightening the room. The light had shot out of me, rebounded off the walls and come back to me, to lie under my tongue and melt there like a sacramental wafer but tastier, holier: starchy and light but sweet like honey, fragrant like rosewater. It was underneath my tongue still, melting there while I murmured my thanks over it, my thanks for the blessing of my new understand-ing. I was like a broken horse who had been touched by the untameable spirit of nature that was its birthright: the stale confinement of my stall could no longer hold me, I knew who I was supposed to be, what I was supposed to be doing. I turned and left the building, leaving the apart-ment building where behind the glowing orange window there were two blessed husks still and quiet on the floor.

I didn't need guidance from street lamps or strangers any longer, not like before, not with the knocking implanted within me. It wound around my diaphragm as I breathed, beat with my heart as it pumped blood. Even if I didn't hear it, I knew it was there, because of the surety it lent to my movements; I could go anywhere I liked on the nighttime street, I knew how to place my feet in front of each other, how to forge a path. Together the child and I would forge my path, the path I needed to take. It would tell me how to move forward. The street was dark and quiet, no passing cars or people, the whole scene sub-merged deeply in those liminal hours before dawn breaks. Those terrible long hours nestled in between night and morning when the foundation of things crumbles, when

the raw skin of the world is exposed. Seated at the threshold in that in-between period I could feel the insolidity of
everything, the way things shake and buzz: the sidewalks
and buildings humming and shivering with obscurity and
it was as though the sun would never, could never rise, like
nothing could connect those hours to the churning process
of temporality, like nothing would ever happen again; like
the world became disjointed from the procession of days
and threatened to be stuck there forever. I floated along
there in the slow ooze of those pre-dawn hours where
nothing exists, buzzing and shaking along with the asphalt
and the stone and brick facades of the buildings, with the
rust of the chain-link fences and the balcony railings, with
the glass of the dark windows, their curtains pulled closed.
My feet slipped softly against the surface of the ground
as I trotted carefully through the emptied labyrinth of the
city, not paying attention to where I was going, trusting
the child to take me where I needed to go without thinking
about it. I hadn't been walking for long when I saw him on
the street just in front of me, with his daughter.

They were the only other people out walking on the
pre-dawn street, standing out against the lonely city and
catching my attention immediately, and as soon as my
eyes touched him I knew that it was him. It couldn't be
anyone other than him. I barely needed to see his silhou-
ette to know; even if all I saw was a decontextualized patch
of skin, a fingernail, a stray hair, I would have recognized

him—we were linked together in a way that surpassed logical understanding, like the mystical bond of twins. He looked like anyone, and could have been anyone, could have blended into any crowd with his anonymous face, his anonymous body, but it didn't matter, I didn't need to use his physical appearance to recognize him. If I had my eyes closed I would know him all the same. My heart sped up, I felt it throbbing in my throat as I swallowed, my mouth dry. He was walking along slowly, hand in hand with his daughter, clasping her hand with that awful hand of his, tenderly clasping her hand with that hand of his that had cracked my collarbone and reached inside to take everything out, that had emptied everything from within me, dug a hole inside my chest cavity. They were just a few strides away from where I was slipping stealthily through the hum of the nighttime world. I watched the girl say something to him in a whiny voice and he responded in a patient, musical tone, to which she breathed out huffily. She was as young and tiny as she had been in the photograph back in the man's house, looking absurd and impossible in the way that all small children do as she walked alongside him. Where were they going at this hour, a young child and her father? They were dressed in respectable daytime clothing, the man in a white dress shirt and black pleated trousers, the girl in a clean little beige dress. The sidewalk below my feet was vibrating, losing the boundaries of its form. The buildings lining the street were fading into the dark sky and then popping out in high contrast, in cycles like breaths, over and over. Everything was on the verge of collapsing, held just back from the point at which it would fall apart. Impulsively I yelled over at the man, but neither of them turned around or reacted at all, like they couldn't hear me even though I was so close to them on the quiet, quiet street. They continued to walk along slowly in front of me, the man lumbering relaxedly as though he didn't know that I had something to give him, that inside me was something that had been created especially for him, that I was nothing else but the vessel for the delivery of this thing.

He was murmuring and chuckling with ease as I crept toward him, and I was the wolf. My eyes were on the back of his head, on the pale, splotchy skin at the rough curve of the back of his neck, at the dark hair spread over his head like little insect legs, sparser toward the crown. Walking carefully behind him I was the wolf; in the fairytale I was the wolf. I didn't look at the daughter, she stayed ostracized to the corner of my sight, almost beyond the scope of my vision. I tried to forget what I had already seen of her. I didn't want her inside my head, I wanted her to remain a vague presence, blurred around the edges, indefinite; a part of the landscape. And the landscape didn't include him; though he walked on the street he wasn't actually touching it, was actually utterly isolated from all the concrete and dirt and aluminum. He wasn't a part of the environment, he was nothing other than himself, a self that couldn't or wouldn't touch the street, couldn't leave his impressions on the city around him. If I looked closely I could see the tiny gap between him and the world, making it so he could never touch, never be touched. Who knew if it was he who had dug the gap or if it was the world, which of them had peeled itself away from the other until the division was total. And it was utterly total—if every drop of blood in his body seeped out of him until he was dry and withered, the blood would never touch anything around it, it would never soak into the sidewalk or stain the discarded trash littering the street; the nothingness around him would simply expand so that no part of him, even after he was dead, would breach the barrier of the world.

I caught up to him: he was directly in front of me. I could have reached out and touched him but still he didn't turn around, his shoulders didn't stiffen, he didn't give any indication that he had noticed my nearness, though of course he must have heard my footsteps on the quiet street; they clopped on the sidewalk like horseshoes against the silence of the night. I could have reached out and grabbed him but I held back for a moment, staring and thinking, readying my pounce, feeling my paws against the cool hard ground, feeling the air as it brushed over my canine body, arching my powerful canine back toward what would follow. I arched

my body toward the future, conjuring its curves and contours, sketching out the shape of its unborn face; I was
birthing the future, using my body to pull it into being.
With each of my small movements I created the moment
after the present, giving form to my destined world. The
man walked across an intersecting street and I stayed
behind, arching toward the future I was creating, prepar-
ing my body, the claws in my paws extending, sharp and
eager against the solidity of the ground. He reached the
other side of the street, continuing to walk slowly with
the girl's tiny hand in his, and I took a small step out
into the road to follow him, extending my leg carefully
forward, my foot softly touching down onto the asphalt,
calling my future into being.

Suddenly, a car ripped into the intersection, just a few
inches from me, nearly scraping me. It stopped right in
the middle of the street, blocking my view of the man
on the other side. The car was boxy, long and tall, with a
square snout and big chrome-rimmed wheels that lifted it
high off the ground. It was painted glossy black, so shiny
I could see my smeared reflection in the side of the vehicle, stretched out like a funhouse mirror. All the windows
were tinted black, even the one on the driver's side that
faced me. Frustrated, I snarled and moved to go around
the car; it edged forward a bit more, blocking my way.
I was about to rush around the car when the dark glass
of the driver's window receded, revealing the person from

the bar sitting behind the wheel. They shook their head at me slowly, blinked deeply with their beady, massive eyes as though I were a pet they wanted to soothe. They were very still in the driver's seat, relaxed back against the dark leather with one hand gripping the wheel. I moved around, ducking and squinting to try to see the man on the other side of the road through the dark passenger window. *You don't want to go there*, the driver said, their voice languorous and flat. Their face barely moved as they spoke, their lips not twitching, their tongue and teeth not shifting; they just opened their mouth slightly and the words dropped out. I stared at them and they were looking back at me with their dark eyes, the purple shadows encircling them. *It's not going to work, going there now. Let me show you something else.* They were tapping their fingers slowly on the wheel, a repetitive, consistent rhythm, looking at me with a face that was expectant but unworried, like they knew I would get into the car with them in the end. I was so tired, my muscles untensing and going slack, the world around me losing its sharp detail, becoming blurred and vague. I walked around the front of the car and on the other side I could see the man further in the distance, still walking at the same steady pace down the street holding the girl's hand. The passenger door clicked and the driver was leaning over from their seat, pushing the door open and gesturing for me to enter the car. I pulled the door open all the way and slipped into the vehicle, closing the door behind me. As I settled into the seat I glanced out the dark window. The man had turned around slightly and was looking back at me over his shoulder.

The vehicle lurched forward and sped off down the street. I turned to the driver; the gaze of their giant eyes was fixed at the windshield, one hand lightly grasping the wheel and the other on their thigh, tapping against their slick, wet-looking pants, some kind of synthetic leather. But they were tapping without any rhythm at all, *taptap . . . tap . . . tap tap tap . . . ta-tap,* on and on with disquieting arrhythmia, compulsively. I stared at their tapping fingers, long with neat fingernails extending out half an inch from the tip, well-manicured and symmetrical, ending in perfect little white curves like bright crescent moons. They swivelled their head slowly from the road to me to look into my face, like an owl, their dark round eyes looking at me lazily without blinking, keeping their head turned away from the road for long enough that my nervous eyes flicked over to the windshield to make sure we weren't about to crash. They turned their head slowly back to the road and stopped tapping against their leg, moved their hand over to the stereo console and clicked a button. Sound flooded the car, deafening and industrial, like the noise of a sped-up factory: shimmering distortion sprinkled over the unending deep, low rumbling of bass, with other tones flicking and twisting overtop of everything. It was synthetic and grimy, like a soundtrack arising from deep within the earth, the part of the natural world where things cease to seem natural: the molten bellow of the beast that's encased under the crust of the planet. It was just as arrhythmic as the tap of the driver's fingers.

I glanced at them and their eyes were firmly on the road but their mouth was moving slightly, opening and closing almost imperceptibly like the silent mouth of a fish gasping for water. I couldn't understand what it was they were doing until I realized they were speaking. But the music was far too loud, filling the car with its screeching, booming noise so that there wasn't room for anything else. I couldn't hear anything they were saying, if they were speaking out loud, if they were speaking to me, but their mouth continued to fall open and then close, the words evaporating in the air as soon as they left their lips, and the music continued to scream like a great big howl of wind, and it was like I was the forest line being pummelled, the branches of my trees wobbling and thin, my roots being pulled up from the dirt, everything being blown away. Like the music was changing the shape of me, was washing away my features so that new ones could be planted within my scarred terrain. I slouched wearily in my seat; outside the windshield the car's bright white headlamps shone out against the blur of the road, the broken yellow lines of paint rushing past like a rhythm,

consistent. Inside me the child was hearing what the driver
was saying, what the music was saying, what the rushing
road and the darkness outside the windows were saying; I
could feel it taking it all in and growing stronger the more
it heard. If I paid attention I could almost feel its understanding moving and expanding within me, a squirming
beneath the skin.

The driver made a turn then slowed the car, flicking a
knob on the console so the music quieted. *Right over there*,
they said. A little up the street was a looming concrete
structure, several storeys high and open to the air, with
pairs of curved hourglass columns distributed along the
floors, holding them up. It looked like a rectangular coli-
seum that had been scraped down to its bones, sleek and
linear and almost delicate, like the skeletal carcass of
some great creature and not just a parking garage. *Go to
the second floor*, the driver said, leaning over me to open
the passenger door; I could smell them when they got
close, pepper and wood and vetiver. The door clicked open
and they floated back to the other side of the car, relaxing
into their seat, gazing at me with their eyes like dark, still
lakes. I looked over to the parking garage; glaring white
lights were embedded into the ceiling of each floor, making the whole structure glow bluish against the night; the
brightest thing in the landscape. There was nowhere else
to go; I unfolded out of the car door and closed it behind
me, not looking at the driver. The vehicle sped off, revving

up to a high speed in seconds, the engine humming with power, tires spinning quickly over the asphalt.

The parking garage was menacing over the street, towering over everything, haunted with the idea of itself, its edges cutting against the dark of the sky, grey and sharp. Everything was being sucked in by it, the concrete absorbing all the light and sound in its environment, making everything darker, quieter; I couldn't see my hands in front of me, couldn't hear my footsteps over the sidewalk, could only see the structure getting closer and closer as I moved toward it. I could smell it as I approached, a wet, ammoniacal scent, like urine and chemicals and rain and moss rolled together, rot and sterility, cleanliness and filth. When I reached the front of the structure I felt the cold coming off of it, too; I put my hand to one of the grey pillars and felt the freeze in my palm, the cold and deadness that ran through the whole structure.

I slipped around the gate arms and walked further inside, where there were endless neat rows of parking spaces, their straight white lines slicing the ground. The spaces were empty, all of them empty, the white lights overhead making everything sickeningly bright, making me squint. The emptiness rubbed up against me, penetrated me, stretched out my insides so that I swelled up with nothingness and silence, so that I started to feel empty like the garage was, like it was excavating me until we were the same. Numb, I moved to the right, where there was a white wall with a door in it. I turned the handle and pulled the door toward me. Behind it was a wide stairwell, the dirty concrete steps covered with trash: empty bags of food, cigarette butts, orange-capped syringes, discarded water bottles with their plastic burned brown. The smell of old, stale smoke stuck to everything while the white lights buzzed noisily overhead, flooding the space with cruel clarity. I stepped around the garbage as I ascended the stairs, moving slowly, my footsteps careful and silent. When I reached the second floor I pushed the metal bar in the door and it swung outward, revealing the same scene as below: cold concrete and endless rows of white-lined parking spaces, white lights glaring overhead and utter emptiness, nothing breaking up the uniformity. I walked through the space looking for what I was meant to see, what I had been directed to understand, finding nothing, just the emptiness that injected itself increasingly deeper inside me, breaking down my tissues, turning me cold and dead like the pillars that held up the cold, dead skeleton I was walking inside of. I walked the whole length of the parking garage turning cold and dead, and when I, nearly frozen, reached the opposite side, there was a person sitting with their back to one of the pillars, head hung slack over their lap, their hair streaming over their face. When I stood a few feet away from them they raised their head to look at me, and the white lights were blazing overhead, and all the sound in the space was soaked up by the concrete, and inside of me everything was stretched-out and hollow. Sitting on the floor with her back to the pillar was the woman I had left back in the apartment. She stared up at me, her hair wet and greasy, her skin sallow, her eyes hooded in darkness, smelling the same as the garage but stronger: ammoniacal, mossy. Under the too-bright lights she flickered a little, like the jumpy numbers on a stove clock, shimmering, and because of this I couldn't see what the expression on her face was—it looked different at every moment, her eyes angry or fearful or blank, her mouth speaking or silent or crying out. She had left the apartment and come here; she hadn't taken the gift I had given her, only pretended to, gone through the motions of it. I had tried to help her and she had shoved my help aside.

I shook before her as she sat flaccid on the floor with her incomprehensible eyes facing mine. I gave up on trying to figure out her expression, letting her face blur before me. My voice rose to a screech and, overcoming the silence of the concrete, the silence of my bloated insides, I asked her whether she didn't want my gift. I wanted my voice to shatter all the pillars, crack apart the foundations, take down the whole structure. I wished that every structure on earth, buildings and mountains and hills, would crumble, collapse, so that there was nothing but a flat, undecorated landscape that my gaze could move across endlessly. If I could have remained in one spot, my

line of sight travelling across to the horizon in all directions without stopping, things could have been other
than what they were. I could have understood things differently, created a different world for myself; the earth
could have been a different animal, and I could have met
that animal differently, I could have lowered my hand to
its nose for us to meet, lowered my head to it so I could
smell the dirt matting its fur, embraced it as though we
were siblings reuniting after a long period of separation.
But the pillars and foundations wouldn't crumble apart
under the force of my screeching voice; the sound just
echoed briefly until it was quiet again, until it was just me
and the woman facing each other in the silent, empty
parking garage, the white lights glaring overhead. She
looked up at me, her face growing and shrinking, shifting, the skin rippling, and raised her hands slowly like a
priest engaged in some solemnly mute religious ceremony.
I stepped closer to her and took her hands in mine, turned
them around so that the palms were cupped toward me.
I felt nothing, letting the motions move through my body,
sent through me by this larger force I had gratefully given
myself up to. I felt my eyes water, tears moving up to
the surface of them and blurring my vision, falling into
the woman's cupped palms, and she didn't move, just
sat still with her hands slack and pliant in my grasp.
There was a pressure growing in my throat and I numbly
waited for it to turn into a sob and escape my mouth, but

it didn't, it grew and grew as I stood with the woman's cupped palms in my hands until it became a tight breathlessness, until I couldn't take in air any longer, and I shook and gasped hoarsely, trying to get oxygen into my body. Weakly, I sank to my knees, croaking and floundering for air, the woman staring at me as I gripped her hands tighter, and then it all began to rise up, from inside me it all began to rise up: the garage's silence that had stretched out my body, the rumbling music from the car and the driver's indecipherable speech, all of it began to rise up toward the woman's cupped palms. I could feel it moving up in me, squirming and thick and alive, moving through my stomach and chest, pushing up into my throat. My head filled with heat and vertigo and I thrashed side to side trying to shake it away from me, my eyes blurring and mucus streaming from my nose, ears ringing, the taste of bile on my tongue. The thing moving up through me pushed into my throat and made its way squirmingly into my mouth, and then its taste mixed with the bile: musty and acrid and pungent, like a mushroom wrapped in coal. I was faint from the lack of breath, sweat pouring off of me, my body shaking and tense, but still I held the woman's cupped hands and she sat motionless before me, letting me hold them. The thing made its way through my mouth torturously slowly as I gagged and retched, and then part of it started to worm past my lips and I could see it, black and glossy and tubular, incomprehensible, a dark slug pushing out of the shell of my body: an eel. It continued to inch its way out of me, exposing more of its body as it hung out of my mouth, and I thought it would never stop, that it would keep sliding out of my body endlessly until the room was filled with it; my brain would shut down, my body would decay, and still it would continue growing out of me, like the hair and fingernails of a corpse. The thing was the length of a finger, and then a hand and then a forearm, and finally I could feel it pop out of my throat, the breath streaming back into me, and heavily it emerged from my mouth, covered in saliva and mucus, and dropped into the woman's cupped hands. From her shifting grey face came a tiny sound, I heard it even through the ringing in my ears: a short little gasp of surprise as the thing touched her skin, and then I released my grip on her hands and she let the thing fall. It splattered, wetly, against the concrete floor.

I was bent over the floor on my hands and knees, trembling and panting, my vision blurry, tears and phlegm and bile falling out of my face. I raised my head and through my throbbing eyes the garage was spinning, but within the spinning I could see the woman squatting with her back pressed against the pillar, looking at her hands stretched out before her. I made an effort to focus, blinking the tears and strain out of my eyes until the scene became clearer. The thing that had left my body lay motionless and banal between us, curled into a thick, wet coil on the concrete floor. The woman looked at me with wide, shifting eyes, her hands held out in front of her, trembling. She opened her mouth and shook her head back and forth slowly. *Burning*, she said, drawing the word out, almost phrasing it as a question, her voice unsure. *Burning*. I blinked and when I opened my eyes again her hands were engulfed in blue fire, the tops of the flames white, coating her hands like she was wearing mittens, and she stood there holding her hands out in front of her, looking at them curiously. She shook her head again as though she didn't understand, and I didn't understand either, and I blinked and the flames had moved up her arms, inching up toward her shoulders, devouring her, and she lowered herself down to the cold concrete floor of the garage, and above her the lights were blazing white, and in between us the coiled black thing lay quiet and unmoving. And I blinked and she wasn't there anymore, all there was was flickering, formless bright blue and white, the heat emanating off of it so strongly that it was making me sweat. The flames were licking and eating in little jumpy curls, moving so quickly, and it was like they were posing a question to me; a question that I didn't know exactly how to respond to, but something inside me did know. I could feel a tickle of recognition at the base of my neck, from the nerves wrapped around my spine, I just couldn't bring the words to the surface of my body. The blue flames had met with the woman and joined her, and from the space that had

closed up in between them and the woman something
new was being created, something that I didn't yet know
how to relate to, how to think of. I sat down on the floor
and waited to see, watched as the colour of the flames
shifted from blue and white to red and orange, getting
smaller, their movements less frenetic, and then the flames
folded completely into themselves, returning home to
that secret place from where fire comes and goes. The air
was impossible in my nostrils, stifling and thick and crude,
but the heat quickly faded from the garage, and soon the
concrete beneath me was cool once more. I traced my eyes
carefully over what the fire had left behind, and my fear
and anxiety rose up in me, making me dizzy. The woman
hadn't been prepared to become something else, so she
hadn't become anything. There was nothing left there,
there was no name that could be used for what was lying
there pathetically on the floor; I didn't have a name for it.

When I exited the parking garage the car was waiting for me just outside the entrance, sitting quietly with the engine off, tinted windows rolled all the way up. I walked over to it slowly, automatically. Somewhere inside me a connection had come loose, a cable's plastic coating had been rubbed off and the frayed wires were disintegrating, energy misfiring everywhere throughout my body: a tugging feeling behind my eyes, a stabbing inside my chest, nerves shooting off signals apropos of nothing. The desperate, insensible movements a body makes when balance has been lost and can't be restored. In the unbalanced rocking boat of my body all the cells were in mutiny, fighting to push each other overboard into the unfathomable emptiness of the sea beyond. I felt as though I'd lost half of my blood, like the insides of my veins were dry but my heart still continued its futile pumping. In front of the concrete parking garage I bent over, retching and lurching, the dirty grey of the sidewalk spinning and twisting. The whole earth was spinning and twisting and I would fall off of it, would continue to fall until I reached deep space, where I'd have to gasp for breath within the endless empty frigidity; not all that different from the cold, empty world on earth that I struggled for breath within. In front of the garage nothing came out of my mouth except thick saliva, dribbling down from my lips toward the sidewalk. The car horn sounded and I heard it as though over a great distance, through layered sheets of glass. The blunt sound barrelled over the distance, finding its way into my body, hitting the barrier of my skin where its waves were sent bounding off in different directions like frightened deer through foliage. And the waves of sound that didn't ricochet off my flesh, that didn't soften and sink, disintegrating, into my skin, somehow found their way serpent-like into my ear, wormed their way into the canal and vibrated those tiny bones inside; they didn't stop there and fall apart, instead they went deeper still, riding along with the electricity that shot through my brain, nestling into a corner of that organ and remaining there, echoing back and forth endlessly, recalling themselves over and over again. Certain corners of my mind were filled with miniscule sound waves like these, living there quietly enough that I couldn't hear them unless I knew what to pay attention to, millions of them living quaintly in the elastic pink landscape of my mind.

Once again the car horn sounded, closer and more pressing this time, and then the hissing scrape of the window rolling down. The sidewalk steadied below me, ceasing to spin and becoming solid as I breathed deeply and rose upright on my weak, rubbery legs, taking staggering steps down the street away from the car. *Did you find what you wanted?* the driver called out the window after me, the words echoing in my head, looping over and over again, *what you wanted, what you wanted, what you wanted.* I continued to move away from them, gritting my teeth at the effort of walking, wobbling, unable to make the relationship between intent and action seamless, a lag between my thought and my steps. The driver said something else, but I didn't know what; the further I moved away the more their voice was faint and unrecognizable, a chorus decaying under a cheap speaker's static hiss. I kept walking, my body falling into a rhythm, my legs beginning to move automatically, without a straining, conscious effort, my ears still waiting for the driver's voice to try to worm its way into them once more, but there was nothing. And then there was the sound of the car's engine rushing into activity, the rumbling friction of tires against the road and I turned around to see the vehicle not trailing after me but looping around in a U-turn and skirting down the street in the opposite direction, the buzz of the vehicle fading and fading until I could no

longer hear it. Then the only thing I could hear was
the drab slap of my dumb feet against the ground and the
shaky woosh of my fragile breath as it pulled and pushed
at the air.

I moved through the city streets unseeing, unfeeling.
I allowed myself to doze just behind my dull eyes, reced-
ing back into my head, curled up behind the occipital
bone like a passenger in a smoothly cruising plane whose
pilot was skilful and kind enough to avoid turbulence or
sudden movements. The child was nestled snugly within
my body and I was nestled within its formidable will, it
within me and me within it, moving together as one, in
step, and the perfection of this seamless alignment lulled
me, pushed me downward through consecutive layers of
sleep: one layer in which the dream was mine, another
in which the dream was the child's, another in which the
dream was the world's, and in all the dreams I was floating in blank space before the child's supreme will, white
walls surrounding us and the child standing in front of
me quietly and with grandeur, a blank, celestial expression
on its face. Nested inside this matryoshka-doll set of
dreams, nothing outside held any significance for me;
everything beyond me was also held within me so what did
it matter, I didn't need to cast my senses outward at the air,
the sky, the street. I let myself dream, and the dream was
cradled carefully in the arms of the child. I gave myself to
the child's will, wrapped myself slickly around it and let it

be the beating heart that determined my place in the world. I was prostrate on the ground before it, asking for it to take control of me so that when I looked upon the world I would understand.

Asleep within the child's understanding I moved across the city, through the last stretches of the night, and when I stopped walking and shifted back into awareness the sun was just beginning to rise over the horizon, the fiery orb just barely beginning to touch the landscape, tentatively lobbing splashes of red and orange and purple paint across the sky, the crowd of buildings on the street waiting patiently for the colour and light to reach them. The child had brought me to a gas station, the white underbelly of the canopy over my head, sharp plastic lights embedded in it shining down on me. In front of me the fuelling stations were assembled like tombstones in a graveyard, holstered nozzles and dull little blank screens. There was nobody else around, the gas pumps standing like mono- liths in an empty desert, and I was standing before them with my mind and body devoid of thought or inclination, just a vessel to be guided by the child.

The child wanted this grimy, volatile amber that had fire living within it, this fluid that was as ancient and frag- ile as the child itself. It wanted to resonate with those ancient and fragile things that the liquid had derived itself from and that still lived within the liquid today, within the cloying chemical substance sloshing around in vats beneath the gas station. The child wanted to place itself into its proper lineage, to harmonize with those things that had, like it, descended upon the world's stage from behind the obscure curtain. But the child had descended willingly, had desired to come and place itself into me to fulfill its objectives here in the world; the ancient things within the gasoline had been forced to, pulled into it non-consensually. Long ago they had roamed the world, had shivered and pulsed and flared before finally sinking into the soft ground, sinking below the depths, encasing themselves underneath layers and layers of crust and rock and eternity. They had been entombed there, coiled tight and breathless in unending rest, and in that tomb were fossils and bones and centuries, millennia, the gargoyle remains and slumbering silence. They slept tight and breathless under the molten crust and calcifying mineral, sequestered away from time's careful unfurling, outside the domain of movement and change.

They had lain there blanketed by that darkness until— flashing, cleaving, slicing through the shadow, rejoining the world to them—there had been the tongue. The tongue, metal and hot and piercing, broke the crust with a crack, thunder reverberating through the earth, reverberating through the ancient things' sleeping place. The tongue plunged itself into the dark recesses, pushing through the veil, penetrating the curtained place beyond the world's stage. It filled everything with its throbbing presence, humming, twitching, mechanical and unthinking. Wanting, thirsting, dizzy with it; buckling and sweating under its hunger, the hunger that constituted its whole existence. It crushed the ancient and fragile things below, pushing up against them, sniffing and probing. With a shaky lurch it licked at them, rushing and whirring, slurping and lapping as everything was sucked up through the tunnel of its throat, a hot river splashing upwards, up through the crust of the earth, pulled back into the domain of time's uncurling hand. And when they arrived there at the surface of the world they became trapped in an inescapable nightmare; billions of hands dipping into them, scooping them up, reaching into them, fingers claw-like with greed. The child sought them, wanted to place its palms on them, to attune itself with those other things that weren't of this world, to learn from them, to take them into itself and free them from their imprisonment. It wanted to take them into myself, so we could free them from their imprisonment, so we could join them to us and to our will, join them to my body.

It wanted to conjoin itself with them, so I was brought to the gas station as the night slunk away to recover its strength and await its next deployment. I took the gas nozzle and grasped it tightly in my cold, pale hand, and poking out the top of the mechanism was the long length of the tongue, drooping sadly, looking like a fear-frozen snake I had yanked out of the ground. The plastic and metal thing sat at the end of my crooked arm like a chalice raised in a toast. Was it my grail?—the tongue didn't squirm, didn't move, only hung miserably from the grasp of my fist, waiting for me to choose it. Was it my serpent?—the child was stirring into movement, knocking against the walls inside me, throwing itself back and forth like it was trying to burst out of me. The chalice shook at the end of my arm but nothing sloshed out over its rim, not yet. But I could feel them in there now, in there and beneath the ground under my feet, beginning to stir and murmur, responding to the nearness of the child, nearness of a thing just as alien as them, just as ancient and fragile as them. They could feel the child feeling them, responding to them, could feel it as it rocked back and forth inside me in excitement. They were there in the chalice, rising up through the chalice, trickling toward the surface, ripples of cold and goosebumps going up my arm, the sun rising up over the horizon slowly, terribly slowly. With the plastic mechanism in my grip I curved my fingers, pulling against the trigger, pulling against the lever that opens the door to the chalice, that opens the door that fills the chalice, that opens the door and lets the ancient and fragile things rush out into the world.

The chalice was in my hand, fluid now flooding over its rim and slopping down my arm, cold against the skin, smelling sweet and thick. The ancient and fragile things came flooding out of the chalice, rushing in a thrashing river, a geyser spilling forth from the depths, and gushing out with them came the fulfillment of my new covenant; new and everlasting. Here it was, what I had been asking for, what I had been wanting: an opportunity to seal the promise, to join myself definitively to something larger than me, something through which I could understand the world, that would tell me how to move my feet, how to blink my eyes, how to extend my hand, forever and ever. With the tip of the chalice I would seal the covenant, would accept the child's command of my will, of my flesh and spirit. It already lived within me, expanding and breathing inside my body, but here was the opportunity to act as its hands on earth, to actualize its will for it, to vacate everything extraneous within myself so that I would become nothing but the vessel for the actualization of its will. To unite it with its brethren, to use my body as the landscape in which it would be united with its brethren, use my body as the landscape on which it would grow stronger, grow fulfilled. I would fulfill it, and thus become fulfilled myself. With the geyser shooting out of the chalice's rim I put my lips to it, cool metallic sharpness against my mouth. The nausea pulsed through me from the tip of my tongue all the way down to my stomach, my mouth numbing, the hazy chemical feeling making my eyes weep and sting. Here was my desert, the place where I would push through the suffering and ascend; through my crying eyes the gas station looked like a mirage, scorched with heat, shimmering in the middle of nothingness. Here was the pain of the rise to the garden, the new and everlasting garden of the covenant.

The taste was overwhelming, dizzying, burning and pungent and thick on my tongue, a sickness rushing through my mouth and throat and head as I tried to swallow, the liquid splashing over my face and dripping down me, drenching me, cocooning me with its harsh smell. With difficulty I forced some of the liquid down into my body, acid rain falling through my gullet into my belly and quickly dispersing through my bloodstream, spreading to all corners of me and then the ancient and fragile things were inside me, resonating with the child, their murmuring voices all entwining together. The child lay still, no longer restlessly knocking against me. I let the chalice fall from my hands and spat on the ground, making myself go quiet, trying to stop the environment around me from spinning and spinning, breathing carefully, trying to listen as the child spoke back to the others, as it ran its hands through them, as it took the fluid into its cupped hands and then rubbed its hands over itself, painting itself with them, absorbing them into itself. Making them all one. And it was over. I had sealed the covenant and could relax into the understanding that resonated out from the child, who would be my guide for as long as we were bound together.

In the distance the door chimes of the gas station's store trilled out happily, two high-pitched, fast notes, *ding-ding.*

The sound cut through the empty dawn, and as it did the murmurs inside me went quiet; I looked over to the store and an attendant was moving slowly through the doorway, his body stiff and awkward as he looked over at me. He was draped in a red polo shirt and wide-legged black pants, all of it too big for his slight frame, spindly limbs dangling out like tree branches. My eyes met his; I wanted to look beneath the mask of his face, to see what kinds of things were floating around in there. And then the nausea rushed through me too powerfully, bringing me to the ground, making my body fold around it as I began to expel a blessing through my lips, as I began to bless the ground underneath me with the byproducts of my covenant. I retched and wept as the child expelled everything that was unnecessary from my body, the fluids slapping loudly against the pavement underneath the white aluminum-and-plastic ceiling, the bright lights beating down on me.

The attendant stood frozen a world away from me, not waving his hand, not moving his mouth, the few feet between us an impassable distance. Nothing could pass between us, no glimmer of recognition: if he were to lift his hand and wave it would be for some other reason, some involuntary twitch of his muscles, some acquaintance or neighbour of his hovering behind me; if I somehow managed to reach out and touch him, the touch wouldn't resonate below his skin, wouldn't pass through to the nerves beneath. He would feel nothing, his face not reacting, his eyes not even focusing on me. I couldn't recognize him, either; as he stood there gazing blankly at me I couldn't tell what he was supposed to signify, what he was meant to stand for. I squinted to try to make it out, to try to read the obscure message etched into him, but there was nothing that I could understand there. I raised my body slowly from the ground, my limbs so heavy that they would surely pop out of me, my body heavier than the earth, so heavy that the whole world was going to fall into it; the attendant was going to fall into it, the canopy and pumps and store were going to fall into it, the world would be ripped apart by my gravitational pull and then my body would fold into itself, my bloated balloon of flesh and feeling would burst apart with a wet *pop*.

The attendant backed up slowly a couple of steps, then turned on his heel and opened the door of the store, the bell chirping happily again. His movements were only half-rushed, only half-serious, like he wasn't sure if this situation was urgent or not, was an emergency or not. He wanted to teeter on the median and not lean all the way in, lest he change things by his own determination, lest the urgency of his own movements influence things. I stood there under the gas station's canopy and closed my eyes, giving myself up, letting the child decide for me where and how I would move. Then I felt my heavy legs lifting and slapping against the pavement, my heavy arms

swinging beside me, dragging the exhaustion of the covenant behind me, carrying it all with me, and when I
shoved open the door I heard the digital bell trill for me,
too. I opened my eyes and the attendant was staring at
me from behind the counter, his phone dumb and quiet
in his hand; in between us was a little rack full of lighters,
a monitor with a bouncing animation of a lottery brand's
logo, a cash register. I couldn't understand what sorts
of things were moving in his eyes, blurred, too quick to
comprehend; but I could see the beads of sweat beginning to form on his face, tiny dewdrops on a quivering
leaf. I hovered atop my stage, far away from everything,
nothing touching me, and the child inside me trilled like
the door, chirping for a short moment like the beginning
of a song, then it fell quiet again almost as soon as it
began. Then nothing else, and the store was quiet and
hollow as I moved closer to the attendant, toward the
counter he stood behind with beads of sweat forming on
his face. And as I reached the counter, inches away from
him, he started to sing, taking up the child's song; little
snippets of sound falling out of his mouth and wafting
over to me, but quiet, undefined and nearly incomprehensible. The child wanted to hear his song so I leaned over
the counter toward the attendant and then hoisted my
body up and climbed to the other side, placing my hands
on his shoulders as he folded under my grasp, falling to
the floor, taking me with him.

On the floor on the other side of the counter the attendant was placid beneath me, his chest rising and falling with deep slow breaths, staring up at me with his dark saucer eyes. From this nearness he was difficult to look at directly; I could barely make out anything beyond his dark eyes, they sent out ripples that blurred the face around them like an optical illusion, his nose and eyebrows and cheeks all shifting and unclear, undulating like the tide. To observe the flat line of the mouth, the starched collar of the uniform, took an extreme effort that quickly exhausted me, so that I would be drawn back to the eyes as a matter of course, like under the force of gravity. I wanted to pop those dark globes out of their containers and roll them around in my palm, study their mechanics, but I was afraid, too; afraid to reach too close to the attendant, unsure how he would react to any of my movements, unsure what sorts of things constituted his being. The child wasn't afraid, it was holding its breath in excitement, fluttering quickly within me like a tender-winged insect, cracking new creases into its understanding like the folds in the cerebrum that increase its surface area, that allow it to contain more and more data encoded within it, more and more until you would think it was filled to bursting but it doesn't burst, never bursts, just sits there underneath its crown of bone. I needed to be a crown just like that, enviously fragile, something that would shatter and scatter its aftermath across the room, leaving an impact difficult to trace, an impact that would squirrel away small remembrances of itself in hard-to-reach places: under the couch, in the tiny crack between the floor and the baseboard. Nothing that you could sweep up and be done with, no—a thing that would slink into the foundations and ensure that the structure never forgot it. That's what kind of crown I needed to be for the understanding that the child wove within me.

The attendant was still singing underneath me but without melody. The notes he hit were unconnected and abrasive and yet unnervingly close to a song, as though the melody were there printed on a sheet in front of him but he was playing drunk and confused, his vocal cords twanging grossly on every awful note. His tune was vibrating through my body, making me resonate with it so that I joined in its creation, so that my bones and skin and mouth were part of the song, so that I was also made liable. The song was directionless, frantic, imprecise, it ran to one end of the piano and leaned its whole weight into it, then scampered over to another spot and repeated it, a stupid dog slipping and sliding over the keys. I wanted to put my hands over my ears and hum loudly to keep the noise out of me, so that it wouldn't enter me and prod at my insides, but the child clapped and clapped at the awful performance and so I bore it, I adjusted to it so that I was clapping as well. Leaning over the attendant I looked deeply into the interiors of his dark eyes, his dog eyes, his helpless and howling and stupid dog eyes, and I felt that he looked up at me through them but I couldn't be sure. I couldn't find exactly where he was swimming inside his dog eyes.

I needed to pull him to the surface, toward me, I needed to open the door at the front of his eyes and lower myself into them so that I could reach that place behind his eyes where he lurked and touch him, and feel him not just in my fingers but deeper inside me; feel him inside the place behind my own eyes as well. The child thought so: we needed something from the attendant that was higher than recognition, higher than touch, higher than love, higher and larger and more elevated, and I needed to fish it out of him and feed it to the child. I lowered my face to the attendant's, closer, closer, close enough that I could taste him, could taste the salt on his cheek as his dog eyes spiralled and glimmered and rippled. The child was in a frenzy, throwing itself around with violence inside of me, making me wince with pain, it was crying out so loudly it made my head ring and spin. A fever struck me suddenly like a bolt of electricity from heaven, terrible and hot and nauseating but strangely uplifting, an invigorating agony that settled over my shoulders and then wrapped itself around me, and through the fever there was something else waiting for me.

I needed to move through the fever to find this thing that was set apart from the banality of the world, this

thing that was an entrance into the inexplicable. I was so
eager. Underneath me the attendant was still and grace-
ful, waiting for what was to come, letting himself be the
blank canvas on which I would paint the future. I moved
my mouth to his and lowered it, his lips fluttering a bit
and then pressing themselves against mine, and then we
were woven together, and if anything were to escape his
mouth it would enter mine, and if anything were to
escape my mouth it would enter his; and here, this could
be a way behind the dark of his eyes. But I still couldn't
feel him anywhere inside his mouth, there was only
warmth and wetness as his breath and saliva mixed with
mine. As he moved his face against me I could feel the
tiny stones of his teeth, the heaviness of his fleshy tongue,
the little goosebumps that dotted its surface. It wasn't
enough. We needed something more, something higher.
I prayed quietly for him to have the courage to do something drastic, to pull the frayed ends of this moment into
something grander, something more final. I prayed quietly for him to take his flat white teeth and press them
into my tongue until the writhing muscle bled, until the
blood dribbled out and we tasted it together, the iron and
heat and tang. For him to keep pushing down as the sup-
ple muscle flicked and squirmed until the whole thing
came off in his mouth; this was what the child wanted,
this was what was higher than recognition, higher than
love: violence. It would be higher than anything else that

could pass between the attendant and I; with my tongue bleeding and heavy in his mouth I would enter the dark of his eyes, all the way in, I would be granted access to his true self, the self that lurked behind the dark of his eyes. But his teeth didn't answer my prayers, they remained hidden and timid inside his mouth, stoic behind the lips that moved against mine. His body stayed limp and useless beneath me, not galvanized by a rush of violence. But I needed it, this highest thing, I needed to open the door to his eyes and drop into the dark, needed to find him.

The child jumped and shuddered with excitement as I took my mouth from the attendant's lips and moved them to his ear so that I could push my prayer into it. There wasn't any way to breach the skin and have the prayer enter him in any meaningful way, to have him hear it in any way that would matter, but still I pushed it up against the boundary of his body as he lay beneath me. I prayed into him that he would take us higher, that he would raise us to the apex from which we could survey the desolation of the landscape below us, and then we could turn away from it, and then we could feast. I told him that he had to take us higher, that there was no other way; that we had to bring it higher, to the climax, as far as it could go, to where it needed to end. And as I prayed into him the child cheered and whooped within me, soaking up the prayer bit by bit as I unwound it, growing more and more heartened with every word.

The attendant was quiet, frozen in place, his knees on the ground and head folded over with his forehead pressed against the floor. I stood over him watching as he remained in place like that, motionless like a fossil, as though he was afraid his prayer would be annulled if he moved. With his still body he prayed to the ground, prostrating himself devoutly to the ground that prevents our endless falling-through the black infinity of nothingness, the ground without which our grotesque bodies would simply fall and fall and fall, would ragdoll through an endless nowhere so purely nowhere it doesn't have any *there* within it, doesn't have even a hint of a possibility of a *there*, so absolutely nowhere that if we fell through it language itself would plummet alongside our bodies, meaning would fall apart and disintegrate under the expansive emptiness of that not-place, flesh and speech becoming equally as twisted and futile, blown apart by that empty space. The word itself, *space*, does nothing to capture what lies beyond the solidity of the earth, far below us and far above our heads. The word leads us astray: *space* but not filled with anything, no air or atmosphere, unimbued with any futurity or history or reality. What's there beyond the safety of the ground is nothing other than the dark underbelly of space, space's horrifically mangled antagonist, the monster that lurks under the stairs without a face and without a mind. The only thing that keeps us from the jaws of this monster is the ground that cradles our feet, that breaks our fall each day that the slumped angles of our bodies tremble against it. The attendant placed his forehead to the ground, praying and begging that it keep him from the jaws of the monster. But that wasn't everything; he prayed for it to also keep him from the jaws of the song, the song whose melody he could surely feel snaking through the room, approaching him with tendrils and roots grasping. The song that had begun the moment the child and I entered the room, that had been taken up in snippets by the child and by the attendant himself, the song that was the flow of the hidden mechanics that propelled the moment forward.

Every moment has a song that pushes it forward, a melody lurking underneath that gives it structure and purpose and direction. If you listen carefully you can hear it, but more than that you *know* it, it's embedded into your very being like a hidden memory that can be abruptly uncovered with a secret word or phrase. Hearing the song is less a process of hearing than it is one of remembering, fishing the melody out from within yourself and aligning your body and spirit with it, dancing to its tune. In the store I didn't contort my limbs or twirl about the room, but I was still prostrating myself to the moment's song, was urging myself to remember it: the song that slathered its presence all over the silent room, vibrating out from the floor and the walls, dripping over the interior of the build-ing like coats of paint applied gratuitously, carelessly, all of it wonderfully excessive. Its force was everywhere, was a part of every aspect of the room, but I needed to pull it out of myself in order to recognize it properly. To propel the moment forward the attendant and I should have been remembering together, but he wouldn't help me scrape the song off the walls and the floor and hold its melody in our hands. He was too frightened by the abandon of it, so he remained facing the floor in his brutal stoicism, praying that the song leave the room and leave him be, that it not snake out of the walls and grab him by the ankle, that it not whip him about the store in wild jubilation. Yet the song would still be unfurled without his participation, the child and I would discover it together, without him, and it would still envelop him whether he wanted it to or not. The song doesn't stop for anyone.

I closed my eyes and let the song tighten around me, allowed its roots to first touch my heels and then to con-tinue crawling upward, let it wrap itself around my calves and thighs without shifting or twitching, not wanting to scare it away before I let its melody soak into my skin, before it could properly take over the room. The tendrils of the song wound around my lower half and I could feel the song in me, the memory of it emerging more and more clearly from deep inside of me, coming into focus, and at the same time I heard it solidifying in the air around me as well, the vocalizations beginning to fill the room, soft hums wafting out from the walls and drifting down from the ceiling like snow. I stood still under the song's winding roots, waiting for the song to fill the room so that I could launch myself joyously into the centre of it, so that I could spin vertiginously within the rhythm's spiral. The roots crept over my hips and my stomach and when they reached up and touched my chest I shivered involuntarily, the song getting louder and louder, the hums shaking the room—and I could remember all of it, I knew how it was supposed to go. There was pressure beneath my skin where the song's roots touched, pressure that wanted to expel itself from my body; it was time for the child and I to join ourselves to the song. I opened my mouth and as soon as I did I felt the song bubbling up in me like heartburn, felt it in my chest and my throat like acrid breathlessness, crushing me; it was monumental, overwhelming, it would suffocate everything in the store. It stuck in my throat, lodging itself there until I deepened my breathing and swallowed, until I relaxed my muscles and calmed myself. Then I was able to push it out of me,

and I let it soar up from my chest to my lips and then into
the air, and when I did that the child immediately took
up the song along with me. It knew the song as well, it
was the one who had encouraged me to remember the
song in the first place. And we sang together: note by
note, I traced the journey of the song with my chest and
my throat, with my contorting tongue and pursing lips
and straining diaphragm, and the child traced the song
alongside me. As I sang the child was there keeping pace
with me, its rhythm matching mine, preceding mine,
guiding mine, correcting mine, since it knew the song
better than I did. The child's adoption of the song floated
right next to mine, like a speaker regurgitating my voice
back to me with a delay so slight it was difficult to hear,
balanced precariously between a perfect overlay and a
clearly demarcated separation, poised on that unnerving
edge. The tension grew as we continued to map out the
song against each other's voices, as the song continued to
fill the room, writhing over the walls and the floor, light-
ing everything up in brilliantly vivid colours, injecting the
space with vitality; the attendant, too, was caught up in
the storm of it, the song danced over his cowering body.
The tension of our almost-aligned voices grew increasingly unbearable as the song continued to unroll, filling
me with restless energy so that I almost couldn't stand it,
so that I was about to break under its pressure and fall
apart; and then the tension subsided. The child's rhythm

faced mine directly, no longer an uneven guide or after-taste of my rhythm but a complement to it. Our voices were two sides of the song, slightly disjointed halves that made a whole, that came together to remember and reflect the room's song more accurately.

It was a duet, and we fell into position to explore the song in a less rigid way. My diaphragm rose and fell, filled and emptied, the room expanding with sound and colour as I sent my melody into it, as I reflected back to it the song that was hidden within it. And the child was there taking up the melody as well, exploring the song from a different angle, trilling and warbling like a flock of birds, my body vibrating with the sound, my blood gurgling and warm. We propelled the moment forward as we sang, our voices twirling over the store, caressing the aisles and the fluorescent lights overhead, our song caressing the attendant as he lay with his forehead pressed against the floor; and then our voices reached the end of the song. In my head I heard the pop and tear of a needle leaping away from a rotating vinyl, and then the near-silence of the store. All that remained was this taut buzzing that reso-nated out from the architecture of the building, a buzzing that I only noticed once the song had run its course. The buzzing had been the substance of the song all along; the song was a passageway that led us here, a way to discover this sound that was the true song of the room. What the child and I had performed was a meandering preamble to the heart of the matter; our melody had been meant only to dig out a silence deep enough that the buzzing could then emerge from the shadows and reach into the room, presenting itself.

It was the kind of buzzing that lurks in the walls and ceilings of all these aluminum-and-plastic buildings, a stretched-to-breaking-point vibrato that spools itself out from behind the layers of plaster and fibreglass, that spirals down from stuttering and shaking too-bright lights, that pulses out from plastic-coated copper wires, criss-crossing the room like an emaciated web. It was the thick pulsing of electric waves, filling the air, nearly visible; if they were visible they would blot out all the light, cover every square inch of the space so that you couldn't see any longer. I could trace the waves back, trace them all the way back to the shuddering mechanisms that birthed them, could see that the forces that created them were none other than the ancient fossils and spirits that coursed through the gasoline in the pumps outside. In a way the buzzing was their song. But the buzzing wasn't just that, wasn't just the electricity lurking in the plastic-coated wiring, wasn't just the power vibrating in the insulated walls of the building. If I tore it all away— ripped the copper out of the walls, tore the plastic antennas off the roof, razed this whole building to the ground—the buzzing would nonetheless remain, per- haps a bit fainter, yet there all the same, floating and phantasmagoric. The song came from somewhere deeper. It was only that places like this allowed you to get closer to it, were more conducive to letting you hear it. The buzzing resonated out from an immaterial place, hiding secret in between things, a language emerging stealthily from the infinitesimal cracks in things that we can't see. And that language was the same language that the child spoke, the same that the ancient fragile things in the gasoline spoke, that the grand will of the world spoke. In the store with the attendant prostrate on the floor I looked at this song, the buzzing that resounded from this secret place in the cracks of reality, and felt the emptiness at the core of it. There was nothing beautiful or substantial about its melody, it stretched itself out barren and ephemeral over the room like a memory of a song, like a shadow that didn't know to evaporate when its subject stepped out of the sun. This was the song that propelled the moment forward, that willed us to dance to it, and it was entirely hollow; it barely existed.

The attendant picked his head up off the floor and pointed it toward me. His skin was damp and flushed but his eyes and mouth were calm, placid, three tiny openings in his face that formed a perfect triangle, evenly spaced and well constructed with each point stark and resolute in its place. It was a strong triangle, one made to withstand force, and I was afraid I would be overwhelmed by its strength, that if I attempted to approach his face the force of that triangle would stop me; its impossible, immovable force. His face was like a great stone wall built around a paranoid city, it petrified me and yet it was so impersonal, it didn't even see me. When he raised his head from the prayer and pointed it at me, this triangle met me, with the dead flatness of its eyes, with the sharp line of its mouth. The rest of his body was still curled into itself on the floor like a quietly taut cat—ready at any moment to uncoil and propel itself skyward. This was where we were after the song had made itself known, this was what the song had moved the moment toward. The attendant was draining the energy out of the room with his dark eyes and sad, stoic face, with the anxious tension of his body as he rolled himself out of his prayer and moved into what would happen next, and I had to take control of the future before he did. The child needed me to take control of the moment before the attendant did.

After he lifted his head off the floor and turned toward me he opened his mouth, disturbing the serenity of the triangle in his face, and asked me what I wanted. *What do you want*, he shot at me as he unwound from his prayer, his back straightening, his body lifting upright from its crouch. He caught me off guard, not only because of his croaking, flat voice, but because it wasn't the right question: there was no melody to it, no gentle and sonorous exploration, it was direct and unanswerable like an alarm, like a weapon. It had me reeling and dizzy, checking myself for exit wounds because I felt the question hit the surface of my body and then pass through it with a quick bang. I wasn't sure what was there inside of the words or what tools I needed so that I could crack them open and find out, so that I could scrutinize the insides and begin to understand; there may not have been anything at all inside of their shells, nothing that would make them more sensible to me. Either way I couldn't know; I took the question and held it in my hands, but when I wrapped my fingers around it and pressed as hard as I could, I still couldn't feel a give, whether my hands were too frail or the words were too dense or just weren't meant to be opened in the first place, whether someone like me would never be able to open them.

There weren't any answers that I could find within me to the question, and I couldn't ask the child; it dozed inside me, lulled to sleep by the excitement of the song, its head rolling on its neck like a lazy pendulum. I searched the room for an answer, looking for something that I could want, my eyes darting over the shelves and counter and cold floor as I waited for something to make my blood pump warmer and quicker, to dilate my eyes and stir in me the hunger that would justify me. What was it that my self, lurking in its sack of oxygen and blood, could want here, in the skeletal aisles of crinkly packaged products? And above them, the unblinking cameras arranged in every corner of the ceiling like perching birds. Perched neatly up in the rafters with their red eyes pointed down watching for meat they could pick roughly off of bones. They surveyed me absolutely and directly, and it was a beautiful relief to realize that I was being watched, because it took away the pressure to find something to want. I became not a self that had to want something, but an object to be regarded; I was removed from my obligations and scooped up instead into another's gaze. In that gaze my self was lost, dissolved like bouillon powder in the soup that's created in the space where a gaze meets its object. I was cleansed, redefined as just a small part of a greater relationality. And when I looked back into the bird's laser-red eye and returned its gaze, the soup between us thickened under a newly enlivened simmer, tiny bubbles breaking the surface as we softened and churned within it. We were now both watcher and watched, making us not two but four, not four but none, not none but an infinity. Our intersecting gazes tangled and knotted beyond com-prehension, so impossible to pry apart that there were no longer any subjectivities between us that had cast the ropes in the first place, only the byzantine web of watch-ing and being watched, being watched and watching.

But I had missed something essential about the plastic birds in the rafters, about the gaze which they directed at me. I had misunderstood what it meant to be watched by them: I felt this with a pang as I became aware of my own dismemberment. As I stood beneath the unblinking eyes of the cameras I was being dissected completely, their eyes were performing this autopsy effortlessly and with-out emotion. With its gaze each camera severed me from myself, took the me that existed in a specific moment and separated it from the forward momentum of time. They took that time-frozen me, that pale shadow, and slurped it into their laser-red eyes, into whatever mechanism lay behind their eyes, and with such a movement that version of me was plunged into an eternity of being watched; an eternity outside of time and space that existed only for the purpose of keeping this version of me trapped beneath the gaze. In that place, behind the camera's eye, there was no escape from being witnessed, there was no variability, no agency, no choice. Behind the camera's eye there was no way to alter this monotonous destiny, in that world there was nothing other than the gaze and the act of being watched.

It was already too late; there was no way to rescue this version of me from the prison behind the camera's glass eye. Every second that I remained in that room another version of me was snipped out of the moment and placed within the plastic bird's cage, the limitless basin of the camera where these versions of me would be subjected unendingly to this immortal, unbending gaze. The attendant's voice surprised me once more, this time closer to my ear: *they can see you.* I looked at him and he was pointing upward, at the cameras in their perches, and a chill went through me at how he had noticed my plight, at his words so loaded with threat and smugness that it was as though he had orchestrated all of this, everything. But he was wrong, the cameras couldn't see me at all, and their inability to see me trapped them so completely that they had to create versions of me that weren't me, not really, that they could watch in my stead. Those snippets of me that existed outside of time and agency were all they could see, they would never be able to bear witness to the breathing animal that I really was. And when I

turned to the attendant and looked into his eyes, I knew
that they worked in the same way: surgically, creatively.
He didn't see me at all, he only blinked and blinked and
severed versions of me from myself, sucked them into the
unknowable mechanisms behind his eyes. Revulsion bal-
looned in me, cloudy and cold, pushing through my gullet and bringing with it its frantic despair. In the end I did
discover something I wanted: what I wanted was to no
longer be sliced apart and restructured by the eyes in the
rafters, by the eyes in the terrible face of the attendant. I
couldn't spend another minute there, being torn apart. I
shot my body forward, leaping toward the attendant to
cover his eyes and put a pause to the tortuous process, but
he flinched away from me, ducking his face into his arms
so that he removed his gaze from me on his own. I looked
back up at the cameras and they stared at me, occultish
and unaffected. The easiest way to stop their gazes from
raining down on me like artillery fire from heaven was to
turn and leave the store.

   As I walked out of the store the door trilled brightly,
cheerfully. The sound didn't wake the child, who was
still slumbering within me. This wasn't the partnership
I had been promised, I was supposed to rest quiet and
assured under the child's supreme will; it was supposed
to guide my hand endlessly, without stipulation. But the
child slept and I was left to figure out what it desired on
my own, despondently. Outside the store the street was

busy, car after car sliding down the road, dirty and chromatic, filling the environment with the persistent noise of their rumbling. The sun was hanging overhead, once again having successfully, impossibly, completed its herculean task of rising up over the horizon, and everything was streaked with red and gold. The cars were all going in one direction, and I walked past the gas pumps to the side of the road and pointed myself in the same direction, moving slowly, lifting my legs with effort and trotting down the street. To the side of me the vehicles continued to rush past, and it was as though we were all moving toward the same destination, and that in their excitement they were sprinting ahead of me, playful and joyous. The vehicles' long, peculiar metal husks were like the defensive shells of insects created to protect the vulnerable flesh within; underneath the cars must have been a dozen thin, hairy legs, fragile but energetic, legs that skimmed the surface of the road so gentle and quick, like a basilisk lizard gliding across water. The beetle-like vehicles skittered as fast as they could down the road in their eagerness, and my legs, tense and tired, could not keep up, could not propel me breathlessly across the terrain. I trotted along on my bloated legs, following the endless procession; I would discover my destination by moving along with their mechanical stampede, limping robotically at their side as they careened down the road throwing up dust and dirt with their rumbling filling the air. Without a thick husk of my own I was exposed to everything; my flesh was so easy to pierce and bruise, the layers of skin stretched over my bones weren't enough, couldn't protect me from danger. I craved something sturdier that I could hoist over my body, a cocoon of tough and tightly woven material that I could seal around me. I wanted to slumber behind the shield of someone or something else; I wanted to live inside some other creature's safety and be free from pain and circumstance. I walked staggeringly along the side of the road guided by the stampede of giant insects, dozens and dozens of them whipping by me with miniature explosions of heat and speed, slicing the air. There was a destination at the end of the road, some cavern they would crawl swarmingly into, and on the inside there would be thousands and thousands of them, husks shining in grey, silver, black, gleaming metal and plastic, all piled up in a continental mound. Magnetically I moved with them toward the end of the road, toward my destination, toward the cavern that I too would crawl into, on my four limbs, low to the ground, and under the spell of the cavern's darkness I would tighten my body into stone and rest for a thousand years until I no longer tired.

The sun hanging overhead, I walked through the desert of the plastic insects' stampede until I reached a point where the road stopped and split in two, with one branch going left and the other going right. Straight ahead, behind the place where the road split, was a large structure sitting

in a wild, untended field. It was a house that had aged
poorly, with cheap wood boards over the windows where
the glass had been removed; a crumbling artifact with
moss crawling over its face, covered in obscure scrawls
and symbols in black and red and blue, like hieroglyphics:
thick letters forming unreadable words, abstract draw-
ings of faces and figures. I thought it must have been the
cavern at the end of the road, where the mound of plastic
insects slept. Between the end of the road and the stairs
at the entrance of the house was an unruly crowd of tall
yellow-brown stalks, as high as my shoulders. I waded
into this forest, sliding through the stalks like a snake in
the underbrush. They chafed against my skin, sought to
scrape everything off me that was dead or dying, to purify
me before I reached the cavern where I would be allowed
to rest. My feet snagged on unseen things—I couldn't see
the ground for the shifting mosaic of stalks that moved
fluidly around me with the subtle breath of the wind, a
frothing river that swallowed my energy as I waded
through it. Halfway through the field I stopped for a
moment and bent my knees, squatting down in the brush
out of the sun. Suddenly I was completely submerged,
crouching at the bottom of a river like a lonely mollusk:
everywhere I looked was the same, identical stalks sway-
ing around me, pushing and scratching against my arms,
my back, my face. I was drowning in them, the air so
thick with humidity that my breaths became increasingly

ragged and desperate until I reached my limit and pounced up again, breaking the surface of the river of stalks. The sun beat down on my head, my forehead and the back of my neck slick with sweat that dripped over my collarbone and down my back. Carefully, slowly, I pushed through the stalks, wading through the rest of the field over to the decrepit stairs and grabbing hold of a banister that shifted unsteadily under my hand.

At close quarters the house looked wild in an organic, inhuman way, like through its decay it had ceased to be something that was created for human occupation and became fully part of the natural environment. Foliage grew through the wooden stairs, popping up in between the steps and around the railings; the building looked like it could have grown up out of the earth, hardly different from the weeds and plants that blossomed around it. I lifted my foot and placed it uncertainly on the bottom step, carefully leaning my body into it. It groaned loudly under my weight, the wood plank bending slightly, but I needed to test its resolve; a step shouldn't protest against the simplicity of its everyday task, against the burden that it was created to bear, that it must bear; it needs to accept its burden quietly, with dignity. I took my other foot and lifted it onto the step, now standing with my whole body on it while it cried out emphatically, insistently, and then the cry suddenly cut out with a loud *crack* and I plummeted, the house rising before my eyes as I sank. Pain shimmied up my leg electrically before settling into a red pulsing concentrated in my ankle and foot. I couldn't see the injured area: a third of my leg was hidden beneath the splintery hole in the stair that I had plunged through. With cautious deliberation I pointed my foot downward and slid it out from the rough hole, then stepped down from the broken step and sat on the ground to look at the wound. The skin was scratched raw around the ankle as though it had been caught in the teeth of something strong but playful that had bitten without biting so terribly hard, just hard enough to communicate the potential of further injury, grazing lightly as a way to tell me that it could have bitten harder, to tell me that it had teeth and was capable of using them. The superficial injury was a warning, I knew as I looked closely at the little strips of skin that had been peeled off me, revealing the newer, fresher skin beneath, pink flesh that burned slightly as the wind brushed against it. Tiny drops of blood rose to the surface in places, not large enough to drip down my legs; I pressed my finger against the gleaming droplets one after another, smearing the thin blood over my leg, and stood back up.

I spread my arms out to grasp the unsteady banisters with each of my hands and distribute my weight more evenly, the ancient wood railings shaking back and forth and creaking, and hoisted myself up, skipping the broken step and stepping onto the second one. The step whined and groaned, but less emphatically than the first one, less committed to its appalled protest, and I quickly bounded up to the next step, and then the next one, ignoring their complaints. I had to prove that my resolve was stronger than theirs by ignoring the bite they had given me, ignoring their screams, continuing upward to the front door of the house, the cavern where I could rest. At the top of the stairs the wood stopped creaking so loudly; the landing only whispered as I planted myself on it, it declined to say anything further. Thus I found myself at the threshold of the house, the front door ahead of me, solid and grand and commanding my respect. Its white paint was chipped and faded and uneven, marred by dirt and with a dozen signatures scrawled and sprayed along it, as though the house itself were a message and these were its co-signers; they had addressed the house to me, and I would have to go inside to read through its contents and receive the message they had left for me. The doorknob had vanished and in its place was a hole the size of a tennis ball. I placed my hand within the opening and grabbed the door, leaning in and pushing so that it swung inward.

I was surprised to find the interior of the house orderly. There weren't any fire-twisted plastic fragments laid out on the floor like murdered things, no unfathomable discarded waste piling up in the open, not even any more signatures on the walls. There wasn't anything at all inside: no garbage or graffiti, no furniture, no shoes or keys, no signs of life or that life had ever been there. But it didn't have the purposeful sterility of a human space, didn't seem like it had been thoroughly emptied and cleaned through a concrete chain of intentional events—it was like the total emptiness of a dream once the dreamer leaves it behind. I was keenly aware that I couldn't be there, that it wasn't possible for me to intrude into the middle of a vacated dream that wasn't my own, and yet there I was, standing in the foyer with blood on my leg, with my fatigued body, with my uncertainty. Through the foyer was a short hallway that ended quickly with a singular doorless doorway on the left. I stepped through the hallway on legs that ached and moved slowly, slower than I wanted them to, my footsteps slapping loudly on the veneer floor but not throwing up any dust; everything was spotlessly clean. I turned the corner and passed through the doorway, and beyond it there was a small room with windowless walls and a light bulb hanging from the ceiling, casting a weak warm glow over the space. Like the rest of the house it was unnervingly bare—though there was a single wooden chair against the far wall, constructed of light-hued oak with a plain squared back, and a frameless mirror stuck onto one of the other walls. There was nothing else, and I wasn't sure how the person sitting in the chair could manage to live in such sparse conditions.

She was wrapped in a flowing, plain black sheet that

went from her shoulders down to her ankles, and her eyes were closed. Or perhaps they were open, it was difficult to tell because of the way she was vibrating against the room. She buzzed in place so quickly that I couldn't make out anything more than a blurred pastiche of a person, like she had been painted onto the canvas of the room by a shaking hand, swipes of shade and colour that were rough and undefined. I thought that she was perhaps asleep in the chair, that this was the dreamer, but I understood she was awake when she unceremoniously rose from the chair in a smooth, gliding motion, serenely lifting herself up while still shimmering like a hummingbird or like a locust. So quick that my eye couldn't quite catch the exact contours of her face as she floated across the room toward me; all I saw was an indistinct mess of shades where her expression should have been, and it strained my eyes to focus on it for too long. She was moving slowly, elegantly, toward me from the chair, the sheet billowing around her, stepping carefully and lightly. Squinting at her was beginning to make me feel like I was carsick, like how straining to focus on the details of the scenery flashing by out the vehicle's window makes your head spin after a while. I blinked and squeezed my eyes tight to try to refresh my vision, and once I opened them the woman was seated back in the chair. It happened so quickly, in the space of the short second when my eyes were closed. I continued to watch her from the doorway of the room, to watch as she again rose from the chair, as she flickered and glistened like a thing hidden in the glow of a candle, as she glided blurrily across the room toward me, and when she came close, so close that I could have nearly touched her, the strain of looking at her once again started to pound too strongly against my eyes, and without meaning to I compulsively blinked hard. It was just a brief blink, less than a second, but when I opened them she was sitting in the chair. I never saw her move back into it, she would had to have moved terribly fast for me not to have seen her. Again: she raised her body from the chair and stepped toward me, toward the doorway, and the nearer she got the more it hurt my eyes to look at her, until she was mere inches from me and I was overtaken by a need to blink; when I opened my eyes she was seated in the chair.

It was like a series of out-of-focus photographs were being projected into the sparse room; they were automatically being cycled through, over and over again: one of her in the chair, one of her standing, one of her walking toward the doorway, one of her nearing the doorway, and then back to the beginning. But I never saw the switch where the cycle reset, I was never able to see her returning to the chair. Because of this cycle she was endlessly attempting to reach the doorway but was never allowed to obtain her objective, moving eternally in a circle, and her unending desire to reach the doorway was what sent her back to the chair time and time again. The

endless loop, the redirection, the entrapment: this was
a scene I had seen before, in a movie, on a stage, in a memory, no—somewhere deeper, hidden beyond the cobwebs
of my twisted recollections, in a place deep inside me,
I could almost see it. This fragile recognition teetered
precariously inside me, I couldn't exactly place it and
couldn't understand why. The woman rose from the chair
again, moving toward me, and I ignored the strain in my
eyes, squinting at the woman's blurred face, trying to
understand why I couldn't recognize where I had seen
this before, trying to understand why the thought flickered in my mind, intangible and hard to grasp, that this
woman might be me.

I couldn't even make out her face, there was nothing
about her that indicated a resemblance to me, but I
couldn't get the thought out of my head, it pursued me
tenaciously without revealing itself to me fully, without
showing me why or how. I couldn't tell for certain whether
there was some truth to the idea because when I tried to
conjure up the image of my own face I saw it in my mind's
eye just as blurry and undefined as the woman's was. I
couldn't recall precisely what I looked like; the fog that
surrounded my self-image wouldn't disperse no matter
how stridently I tried to blow it away.

I went over to the wall of the room where the mirror
was hanging; the glass of its surface was old and distorted,
with streaks of smoke and grime discolouring and

obscuring it, like there was an eternal storm lingering
inside it. When I walked closer to the mirror I entered
the shadowy part of the room, outside the orb of light
cast by the bulb hanging overhead, and when I entered
the shadow the child inside me finally stirred, finally
began to awaken from its nap. It turned restless and
started to fidget like it was disturbed, like it didn't like
what was going to happen. I looked into the cloudy mirror and through it I could see the woman still moving in
her loop, rising from the chair and moving toward the
doorway before reverting back to the chair; I could see
this in the mirror but still couldn't see the exact moment
when she was returned, couldn't see by what mechanism
she wasn't allowed to reach the doorway. I continued
to stare at her glitching cycle through the mirror, and
beside her, reflected there, was my own face; I moved my
eyes slowly over to it so I could study it, so I could
remember it, so I could understand why being near it
infected me with a horrible fear. I didn't want to look at
it; my eyes slid toward my reflection so slowly and I had
to fight to stop them from looking away from the mirror.
When I finally looked at myself the child screamed, wail-
ing mournfully as it tossed itself around inside me, and
the child's tantrum alongside my own fear created this
great blood-chilling rumble inside of me that stabbed
my abdomen, sending spasms through my stomach and
torso. In the mirror my reflection was gagging and

coughing, gagging and coughing as its eyes met mine directly, and tears were rising in the red, tired eyes and leaking out the corners. I had forgotten what I looked like, and the shock of seeing and remembering made my heart seize with fear, with terror, as my reflection continued to shed tears out the corners of its eyes, as the child continued to wail and throw itself around. Behind me in the mirror the blurred woman was frozen in the middle of her cycle, no longer moving toward the doorway; she was standing beside the chair very still, turned toward me, her indefinite face watching with what looked like curiosity.

The fear abated for a second, just a quick moment where I was vacant of feeling, and then the horror began to descend over me. It began its descent by first touching the crown of my head, gently and chillingly, and then dripping downward, over the lids of my eyes, the lobes of my ears, over the tender skin between my nose and mouth; it dripped down over me but I would not let it be mine. Such a horror was not mine to face, because an animal isn't fated to bear such horror, an animal doesn't feel shame or loss or resignation, all it knows is its hunger; and here was my animal flesh, pale and scratched and bleeding, here were my animal palms and animal feet, here on my face was my animal mouth, my animal eyes. I could taste my animal essence beneath my thick tongue and clinging to the roof of my mouth, and when I tasted it the child calmed. I was the animal that carried the world within me, just like every animal carries within it the thing that will surpass it in waves; with the child carried inside me I surpassed myself in waves, I spread open my animal hands to receive everything I needed and to become all that I needed to be. And what I needed to be was enough; everything tangential to my purpose pushed against my walls, wriggling to get in, but I wouldn't let it taint me. Nothing would remove me from my singular purpose, I would not avert my gaze from its dazzling presence, I would not let anything else catch my gaze. I would not let the horror become my own. In the mirror my reflection was still and quiet, no longer shedding tears, and behind it the blurred woman had reverted to her loop, but with her smeared face still fixed on me; in her inscrutable face a vast mystery was winding itself around and around, strong twine looping around a gift.

I bounded out of the house, leaving the woman and the mirror behind me, rushing through the hallway and then taking hold of the front door and throwing it open so that it flapped feebly on its brittle hinges. When I felt the cool air on my skin and the wood of the front porch under my feet, I didn't think, there were no thoughts in my mind, and in the void left by my thoughtlessness there was only the singing of my rushing heart, a song that propelled me into the air, shooting me above the splintering planks and shaking railings. I jumped off the porch, and for a moment after I was launched into the air I was untethered to anything, not to the ground or my thoughts or my self, and the euphoria of complete disconnectedness made my whole being swell with heat and joy like the dawn breaking over the horizon. I was briefly suspended completely in the thick ooze of the present, unrelated to the earth or the forces of the air or to my own corporeality; there was nothing except the present moment stretching itself out taut like a thick elastic and the gleeful singing of

my heart. I waded in the sickly sweet goop of that lone-
liness for a millenium, the present stretching itself out
forever, a thousand years in a second as I circled around
and around like cool water surrounding a drain, the
hapless drain pulling at me and pulling at me but not
managing to send me anywhere. Then the moment was
over: I was thrust through the confines of the present
and sent thundering into the future, and the future
was the solid ground reaching up to meet me as I fell.
I landed hard on the same leg that the step had already
wounded and my body curled up at the foot of the
stairs, my spine curved elliptically around my knees.
The pain shot from the bottom of my foot into the
crown of my head, a quick creature made of fire sprinting along the length of my body.

The stalks in the field were waving softly in the breeze—
golden, earthy, sun-scorched and dirt-kissed. The sun
overhead had become even hotter, beating down on me
as I lay on the ground. I righted my body and leaned into
my knee to stand up but the pain exploded electrically
again, running laps inside me, touching everything, flicking on neon lights in every room of my body. When the
wave of pain passed I looked down and saw that it wasn't
my calf at all, which was still covered in a tender layer of
dried blood but otherwise normal. It was my foot that was
sitting at a peculiar slant, the mathematics of the angle all
wrong. The child had gone back to sleep, I couldn't feel its

will guiding me, I would have to command myself in order to pass through this situation. Inside me there was no motion I could sense from the child, no language I could sip at, there hadn't been anything since I'd left the room with the mirror. I cautiously turned onto my stomach and stretched the injured leg out behind me, the twisted ankle lifted into the air, a glass raised in a toast like the field was my banquet hall, the stalks my eager guests. I began to crawl over to the road, back the way I had come; I had left a kind of path through the brush on my way in. I kept the hurt ankle off the ground, leaning into my three sturdier limbs, head down and huffing like a dog with my forearms scraping and pulling along the ground, my bruised and battered knees dumbly following. The ground beneath the golden stalks was rough and it left its marks on every part of me as I crawled over it, biting and scratching at my legs and arms and stomach, breaking through my clothes, attacking the skin, going deeper, the landscape etching itself onto my very bones, tucking mementos of itself in between layers of fascia. I could feel it imprinting onto me, could feel the pain and discomfort of the crawl seeping beneath my skin as my limbs scrabbled against the ground, as the dirt embedded itself in my palms and under my fingernails. I was trembling, bubbling over with the cold burn of my anxiety, my mouth drying up and vision blurring as dark clouds of dread took over me. This wasn't the contract I had made, this wasn't how it was supposed to go; I wasn't supposed to be alone. My broken ankle throbbed red and unsteady in the air behind me like a flag of warning, but it should have been bleached white in resignation, or in surrender.

I was deep in the tall stalks like a serpent swimming through the grass, but there was nothing silken and poetic about my movements, no beauty like there is in the dance of a serpent. I didn't know how to channel my serpent's dance, and instead my movements ached across the stage without beauty, without grace. I was hidden there in the filth, in the dirt, so low and sequestered that the sky couldn't even see me if it tried; when I looked up the sky appeared through the ripples in the reeds all broken up, shattered and shifting like I was instead looking down into the depths of the sea, through the algae and excrement and shadows of fish, and suddenly I didn't know which way I was facing or where I was supposed to go from here. I didn't know why my body was trembling and aching and broken on the floor like a tree felled in an indifferent forest; something had set its sharp teeth into me but I didn't know who or what, I didn't know why I had been felled, whether I was about to be shredded into pieces by the mouth of some brutal machine. I was supposed to align myself to my singular purpose, to throw myself at the feet of it, but it wouldn't even guide me anymore. The will of the world refused to whisper into my ear.

As I lay there decaying in the dust, unsure where I was or how I should move forward, a cry slipped through the reeds and made its way to me; a powerful cry like the call of a deep-throated bird, sounding over and over again, filling the space. I cracked my body open and rose up onto my forearms, starting to pull myself through the parched foliage once more, letting the sound guide me, following it to its source. My arms dragged against the dirt, my neck and shoulders aching and sore, my stomach tense and straining, the stalks harsh against my skin and obscuring my vision, so I couldn't see where I was going as I pulled myself toward the sound. After several moments the stalks thinned and suddenly there was the road, and on the road the driver was standing beside their car, leaning into the open door and pushing on the horn to make the giant machine shriek. I shrieked back at the car, yowling with the animal pain that was exploding in my body. The driver let off the horn and walked over to me, their footsteps clicking on the ground, closer and closer, until they stopped right in front of me and I could look at the shoes in detail: they were made of dark leather spiderwebbed by rich mahogany veins, the leather letting off a wet, vital smell—not calfskin, something else, it smelled too different. The boots were slender and ended in a squared toe, with a tall heel sculpted like the body of a centipede, a column of intersecting trapezoids matte and dark and solidly smooth like glass. As I looked closer at the heels I could tell there was something etched into them, tiny script winding around the blocks, but I couldn't concentrate enough to read what was written there because of the pain and confusion in my head.

The driver, looking down at me, despondent and bruised on the ground, asked what I was doing. I told them I didn't know, the words gurgling low in my throat, tossing around in the rolling boil of my blood; I was still belly down on the road, straining my neck up to look at them and the sun was behind them beating hot and bright down on us, heating up the asphalt of the road so that it was searing against my skin. The driver lightly scuffed the toe of their boot against the ground, out of impatience or boredom, and looked me over quickly: *where's the gift I gave you back at the bar . . . ?* Then, before waiting for my answer, they shrugged and turned around, walking back toward the vehicle. *Get in the car.* I gritted my teeth and started to pull myself along the coarse asphalt of the road on my scrabbling, crawling limbs, and the grit of the road's surface was like a mill grinder, like a sieve, scraping off all my skin and sweat, grabbing violently at my flesh, reaching for the blood that simmered beneath the skin, wanting it to pour out. The hot black rubble of the road was sulphurous and fissured and I could pull it apart with my fingernails, I could turn my hands into spades and dig and dig but never, ever find any bottom to it, never find anything

underneath other than more asphalt, endless, noxious
and heat-packed all the way down to the core of the
earth; and then I would find that the core itself was just
another impenetrable mass of petrol and waste, that its
toxicity was what kept the earth around it belching,
vibrating, alive. There were scrapes on my knees, scrapes
on my elbows, there was phlegm sticking in my throat
as I dragged myself over the hot asphalt toward the car:
the passenger door was wide open, facing me, and the
driver was sitting in their seat on the other side, reclined
comfortably with a vacant expression on their face, the
lengthy fingers of one hand hooked over the rim of
the steering wheel. I was just a shadow stretching itself
across the ground, I was seeing the world from the van-
tage point of shadows, of discarded things and of insects.
Peering up at the driver from below I could see the underside of their tiny, slim chin, the waning-moon nostrils
beneath their nose, the unblemished, smooth skin that
hung over their cheeks, over their brow. Their eyes flicked
mechanically over to me as I stared at them, and they
jerked their head to the side, motioning for me to get into
the car: *let's go, it's time.* I had made it to the car, the heat
of the asphalt spreading through my whole body like
I was on fire. I raised my upper body off the ground, a
deep-sea creature breaking through the tense surface
of the ocean, and reached my arms up, grasping for the
leather of the seat with my animal claws until I felt

the cushion of it under my fingers. I leaned into the seat and hoisted myself up, my breath ragged, feeling my heart and lungs clank and stutter inside me, an ancient engine underneath the veil of my skin.

I lifted my hips up and swung my legs into the car, the seat warm under my thighs, and sat there shaking in breathlessness and pain. The driver leaned over me to pull the door closed and it snapped shut with a muffled little bark, like the surprised hurt of a kicked dog, and they looked me over again with their emotionless reptile face: *what happened to you?* I pointed toward my foot, trying to explain in brief spurts of confused words: my foot, the house, the wood, the porch. The driver flicked their eyes over to my foot and then back at me, unreactive, their tiny straight mouth unflinching, big saucer eyes unblinking, and I looked down at my feet to find that they were both normal: my legs were splayed out at the bottom of the car, shivering and dirty, with streaks of dried blood painted over my left calf, but at the bottom the feet angled out in the typical way, with neither foot pointing in a bizarre direction. I tried to move the injured foot and found that I could rotate it in a circle easily, that I could wiggle it and make it obey my will without tension or effort. The injury had vanished as though it had never been there. This discovery brought the blood away from my head, I could hear each tiny movement of the environment as though it was amplified; could hear the driver

as, in a series of quick motions, they retrieved the key
and plunged it into the ignition, twisting it sharply and
thrusting the shift into gear, the car crying into power. I
could imagine the vehicle's happiness—the simple joy of
a machine subsumed in activity, the simple joy of a thing
synonymous with its movements, a thing for whom every
moment exists as a pure exploration of its purpose, of its
reason for being. For a machine, existence is an unadul-
terated form of playful curiosity, and I needed that too;
that was what I had been promised. I watched the driver
swing the car into motion, interfacing with the pedals
and the shift and the wheel, watched them become a
part of the machine as they took control of its motions;
watched them become absorbed into the machine as
they commandeered it, becoming just another append-
age used to assist the machine in its investigation of its
own intrinsic power.

As I sat crumbled and defeated in the passenger seat
with my body half-turned toward the driver, I could
sense something in the shimmering corner of my awareness, something lingering there in the back seat that I
could almost see but not quite, that flirted at the edge of
my vision hinting at itself. It was like I knew what it was,
like I both knew and didn't know, and I didn't want to see
it; I didn't want to have to know for certain, to be con-
fronted with that reality. I turned my body away from
the driver to sit facing forward and let my head loll, chin

against my chest, and pulling my legs up onto the seat to hug my knees, rolling myself into a ball. The driver tapped their long fingers on the steering wheel, looking straight out the windshield at the road. The procession of cars was gone, there were no other vehicles driving alongside us.

We drove, the road accelerating beneath us and the horizon racing endlessly toward us without ever getting closer. Sleep attempted to take hold of me and I fought against it, tightening my muscles to try to get blood flowing quicker through my body, breathing deeply and attempting to focus on the landscape outside the car: the endless sameness of the rushing road and on either side of it the overgrown fields of green and yellow and brown, the abandoned and decaying structures. I told the driver that I wanted to be taken to see a doctor, that my body was overworn to the point of collapse, that I could not continue to go on and I needed to be changed, I needed something to be different, to be made new. My body needed to be created anew. *We're en route to a hospital*, the driver's mouth barely moving and their hands yanking harshly at the shift stick as the car's speed increased, pulling and tugging at it as though they were sparring with the car; *you have an appointment*, their eyes snapping coolly between the road and the mirrors, not looking at me. I tried to keep my eyes glued to the world outside the windshield, concentrated on the horizon as it rushed toward

us, but through the fatigue my mind still fizzed and simmered with the flickering awareness of whatever was
there in the back seat, with the dim comprehension
that there was someone sitting there, directly behind
me, and that it was all awfully, terribly familiar to me.
Whatever it was, it was intimately, pressingly familiar to
me. Out the windshield the flat landscape was trans-
formed by our driving from a solid place into a fluid roar
of speed and motion, the alchemical rituals of the vehicle's burning rubber and firing engine transmogrifying
space into time, magically, esoterically. The driver's long
fingers were gripping the leather of the steering wheel,
with the hard bones at their knuckles poking out, and
their hands were like the preserved skeletons of some
rare bird, the remains of a species mysterious to all except
the most learned biologists. I asked the driver what my
appointment was for as their hands wrestled again with
the gear shift, shoving it through the corners of its tiny
labyrinth; a shard of sunlight pierced through the windshield and hit their eyes directly and they did not squint,
they did not scrunch up their face or move their head
away. *It's time*, they said simply, and the words tore open
my flesh and began to feast on my organs, the words
rabidly clawed my insides out of my body with the
fiendish desire of making me empty inside, completely
empty. It wasn't true, it wasn't time yet; they had to be
mistaken, I wasn't ready, not ready to be on my own. The

child had only fallen into a quiet slumber, it needed to recover its strength so that it could articulate itself once more, so that it could take hold of me once more. I had just accepted my charge, my blessing, and I couldn't be left alone again so soon, left to choose on my own again. It wasn't time for it to be over, I needed more.

And in the back of the car I could still feel someone there, some kind of shadow rustling around in the back seat; the nearly invisible little hairs on the back of my neck stood quivering to attention, my skin going cold and clammy. I could feel him hovering there right behind me, could feel his face floating just behind the headrest of my seat, I could feel the moisture in his mouth, the warmth and bacteria that wafted up from his thick tongue as he breathed out. I could feel the gurgle and growl in his throat as he dropped open his mouth to prepare to speak, and it was like I knew what he was going to say, like it had already happened before, like it had been gradually happening for hours and hours. I moved slowly in my seat, twisting my body around to face the back seat compulsively, no longer able to contain myself, needing to see his face before the words burst from his humid, foul mouth, needing to know, and the driver's hand clamped down on my arm, gentle but firm, stopping me before I turned around fully. As soon as their hand grabbed me my energy vacated me completely and my body melted once more, deflating into the passenger seat

as the driver's emotionless face told me to pay attention
to the road because we were nearly there.

The road was the same as ever, the blur of asphalt
and on either side the bland earth, the weeds and grasses
and abandoned buildings. Up in the distance was an
intersection with a traffic light hanging overhead, and
the cables it hung from were covered by a roost of small,
nondescript birds; the traffic light was shifting ever so
slightly back and forth under their talons, back and forth
over the road while the stoic little birds looked over at us.
The signal was malfunctioning, stuck on yellow. The
driver slowed down as we reached the intersection and I
watched the yellow light swing back and forth slowly
over the road; there was nothing else around us, no vehicles approaching. The driver flicked the lever beside the
steering wheel and made a turn. The birds remained
quiet and unmoving on the wire.

After we turned, the sparseness of the landscape slowly
started to give way to clusters of squat buildings, boxy
and red-bricked or aluminum-sided. The sides of the
road shifted from unkempt fields of thirsty foliage to
slim pale-grey slabs of sidewalk, but there weren't any
pedestrians walking atop them: no one sweating over the
pushbar of a baby carriage, no one's dusty boots slapping
against the ground as they walked, the dirty soles splitting away from the ancient leather. There still weren't
any other cars, either, like it was the middle of the night

with the sun burning overhead. As we entered the town
the driver began to hum quietly under their breath, a tune
that I wasn't familiar with, and sat up straighter in their
seat with both hands gripping the steering wheel. The car
slowed and the buildings out the windows clarified into
detail: an old three-storey apartment building with rusty,
corroded balconies sagging off of it, about to collapse;
pulsing neon text in a window advertising accounting ser-
vices; a corner store with all its lights off, the faded sign
bearing the owner's name alongside *lottery, tobacco, cold
drinks*. Up ahead in between the buildings was a wide
curving driveway of crisp black asphalt, several shades
darker and cleaner than the pothole-marked, crumbling
road, flanked by healthy-looking grass that was deep
green and impeccably trimmed. The driver gently guided
the car off the road onto the driveway, and once we'd
turned I could see that it spooled out lengthily into the
distance, all the way to the horizon. Far in the distance
was a large building that could be seen clearly because
of the flatness of the landscape and lack of anything else
that could draw attention away from it, no spindly trees
or clustered outbuildings or rolling little hills, just the
stark singularity of this building, undeniable and absolute
above the driveway and the short, well-maintained grass.
It was constructed of three massive rectangles stacked
asymmetrically atop one another, so that they didn't align
perfectly and their edges jutted out from the sides; it was

grey, blue, silver, gleaming chromatically in the sun, the sides adorned with many thin columns of metal placed randomly, like cell bars that had been sliced off and then glued back on hastily, without any order. There must have been thirty floors: the building loomed over us like a strange monolith that had fallen from the sky onto the lot.

The car drifted slowly along the driveway that wound on and on through the massive lot, the building getting closer and closer and the driver stiff and attentive, sitting straight up in their seat, until it was directly above us. We rolled to a stop under a canopy that jutted out from the building, thin steel slats layered under a large sheet of glass that was textured in a way that made it seem like it was always raining. The entrance to the building was right beside us, and its wall was made of the same large panes of distorted glass as the canopy, and through them I could see the blurry shapes of objects and of people moving around, but couldn't make out any details beyond the shadows. In the centre of the entrance were two giant panes of glass that split apart at the middle to allow you to enter the facility. There was something wrong with the sensor, it was too sensitive, and while the car idled the doors kept opening and closing in an unending, cyclical motion, like the gentle wings of a large bird, so that through them I could see inside in snippets: could see everything painted the brightest shade of white, bright white that nearly glowed fluorescently, the walls, floor

and ceiling all blurring together as though I were snowblind, blurring too with the white desk that was stationed
in the entryway, behind which a woman stood still, her
ponytail taut against her hairline, pulling up the skin
of her face. The woman looked up toward our car and
the doors slid closed again. The driver took their hands
off the wheel and jerked the parking brake, twisted the
key out of the ignition and got out of the car, closing
the door firmly behind them. The noise of the door closing remained floating in the air of the car, echoing around
softly, and then it was very quiet, so that in the back seat
behind me I again began to notice the presence of someone hovering there, his breath close to me, the fabric of
his clothes shifting against the leather seat as he moved
slightly, heat coming off of him. He was about to say
something, I could feel his rancid mouth begin to move.
Then the driver pulled open my door and without
thinking I twisted my body toward them, and they hooked
an arm beneath my legs and another around my upper
back, and pulled me up out of the car. I let my body flop
tired and resigned in their arms like the wounded animal
that I was, surprised at their strength. They closed the
passenger door with their foot and began to carry me
over to the entrance of the facility, and I couldn't hear
their breath or their heartbeat. I lay limp in their arms
and closed my eyes, like a child being carried to bed, and
heard the mechanical slide of the door as we slipped into

the building, then I was like a fish floating serenely in a
dentist's tank, suspended in the light and meaningless
ambience: the flashes of light and shadow against my
closed eyelids, the muffled sounds of people and machines
in my uncaring ears, the feelings of gentle motion as my
body was carried through the hospital.

When I opened my eyes again a story was unspooling
itself around me, a story that didn't concern me and yet
nonetheless stretched itself over my tired body. A woman,
not the same as the one who had been standing behind
the front desk but with a similarly taut ponytail pulling
up the skin of her face, stood in front of us in a bleached,
baggy uniform that was composed of layers of different
items: robe, jacket, vest, shirt, undershirt, pants, dressed
as though she were departing on some sort of dangerous
expedition, her protective layers meant to defend her
against the elements. Without exchanging a single word
with her, the driver lowered me into a wheelchair that the
woman held steady, her hands firm on the chrome handles protruding from the top of the seat. I kept my body
relaxed as I was placed into the chair, letting myself melt
into it; the arms were cool when I rested my hands on
them, the air smelled vaguely like bleach and soap, and it
didn't make any difference whether I kept my eyes open
or closed. All I needed to do was be limp and yielding and
things would unfold around me; all I needed to be was
the placid, easy reader of the story. The child still didn't

move inside me, I didn't feel the blessing coursing hotly through my blood, inside I was perfectly empty; the perfect emptiness of a thing that was created to be empty. Behind me the woman stepped on a lever and leaned slightly forward, pushing off and propelling us into motion, and the walls were so completely white that they looked the same whether they were still or rushing along, my eyes gliding smoothly off them like they were made of ice. I closed my eyes again, hearing the roll of the chair's wheels against the ground, the slight squeak of its mechanism, the even rhythm of the woman's practised footsteps, careful and quiet like the steps of a deer on soft earth. We didn't speak, only moved purposefully through the complex, turning one corner, then another, my eyes peeking open and then falling back closed. Every part of the building was indistinguishable from any other, slick and bright white; I was hapless in a blizzard, I held my breath and cleared my head of thoughts, drifting through the storm calmly and indifferently. People passed by as we moved through the facility: long white jackets, purposeful, trained footsteps, eyes locked straight ahead, I saw them in glimpses every time I opened my eyes but they never looked back at me.

The chair slowed to a stop and the woman pushed the lever at the bottom, locking it into place, and moved in front of me. I looked carefully at her, opening my eyes as wide as they could go and trying to focus, but she looked like anyone, like no one—when I shut my eyes again the image of her face wouldn't surface through the murky waters of my mind, only the starched layers of her uniform and the vise of her ponytail. She cleared her throat lightly and nodded at me, then slipped through a doorway, sliding the door almost all the way closed, and disappeared. The door was the same white as the walls, with no window, handle, or latch, and beside it was a little circular interface, dark and glassy with a glowing red dot in its centre. I couldn't tell if it was staring at me or if I was meant to press my finger against it in order to cause some effect. The woman had left me in a small room, austere like a cell, darker than the rest of the facility; the only light came from the hallway, shining in through the crack in the sliding door that she'd left ajar. The only thing inside the room was a bed, pressed against the furthest wall from the door, hip-level off the floor with a thin white sheet stretched over it, a tiny flat pillow at its head. I looked around for a switch on the wall that I could flick to brighten the room, but there was nothing that marred the perfect whiteness other than the red eye beside the door. The chair trembled a bit as I rose from it, planting my feet on the plain white floor that shone smooth and glossy. I could feel the cold rising up from the floor as I took two steps toward the bed, my body aching and desperate for rest. I grabbed the edge of the bedframe and swung my body up so that I lay on my side on the

thin mattress; it was so thin that the plastic frame underneath poked and prodded at my bones, I felt the pressure
of it on my hips and shoulders as I tossed around trying
to get comfortable, and then lay still on my back, my
body straight out and stiff with my feet nearly touching
the white plastic barrier at the end of the bed.

The fatigue was rising up from my chest and unwind-
ing itself through my whole body heavy and indisputable,
pulling me down, down into the bed, clogging the insides
of my ears and holding my eyes shut—and then I was falling backward. I was falling backward endlessly because
my body couldn't touch anything, couldn't reach anything below me, not the sheet or the pillow or the bed, I
hovered over them at an infinitesimal distance, falling
toward the fabrics but never sinking into them. I realized
that my skin, too, wasn't able to touch my clothes; it was
obliged to keep the tiniest distance away from the fibres
and threads, a distance that was impossible to see or
touch but that was nonetheless there. This tiny, unnotice-
able distance was there even inside myself, even separating
my body from itself—it was there in between the bones
and the muscles, the veins and the blood, the pupil and
the iris, everything was held just ever so slightly apart
from everything else; nothing touched. This impassable
distance exists at every place where two things meet or
where a thing meets itself; it exists even at the smallest
possible aspect of a thing, at the microscopic level, an

irrefutable gap that nothing can ever breach. The empty space surrounds each pinprick of matter like a moat, ensuring that nothing can ever really touch me, that I can never really touch anything else, that there isn't any touching, any breaching of the boundaries. That moat isn't empty, though; the gap between all things isn't true emptiness. There's something lurking there in the emptiness, and I saw it as I lay there in the bed falling backward: an animating force, a thing that desires, that wills, that pushes at every pulsing atom, that keeps everything trapped in the confines of its form. A volition working tirelessly to keep everything apart, to stop everything from melting into everything else, from ever truly touching. This understanding descended on me as my exhausted body fell backward into the hospital bed, like a blurry photograph developing into sharp detail until with gasping breath I saw it, saw the presence that lurks there in the emptiness between all things. I could see it clearly behind my closed eyelids, I could hear its voice resonating through me, and when I saw it this presence reached up toward me from inside the empty gaps in between all things, grabbing at me, wrapping itself around me, pulling me down into its world, into its dream. And then I truly fell backward, fell backward into the space that exists in between everything, into the dream of the will that upholds the boundaries of all things, the dream of the will which articulates the separateness of all things.

I fell backward into the emptiness in between all things, backward into the place that is the dream of the desire to keep everything apart. As I fell the force of that desire was wrapping itself around me tightly, a thick muscular coil of serpent whose strong grip I felt deep in my bones, crushing me totally, crushing me so that it could take me and rebuild me. Under its grip I relaxed, my muscles releasing softly, giving myself up to it. Everything around me was hazy and uncertain and yet familiar; I hadn't been there before but the place had always been with me, hiding in the walls, hiding beneath the ground, hiding under my fingernails, concealed inside of me. The veins of that place criss-crossed through all things, hidden like a mining shaft beneath the surface of the world, beneath the surface of our minds and bodies, behind the curtain that sits next to the world's stage. Peel back the veneer and it's right there, as obvious as anything else—more obvious than anything else, more real than the dirt or the soil or the plastic, than the gases diffusing over our heads, than the enormous ball of light hovering in the sky and diligently burning itself alive. All these things, in spite of their solidity and their powerful presence, still bend dutifully to the will of this emptiness; everything on earth and beyond it prostrates itself before the dream that upholds the separateness of all things, the dream of not being touched, of not touching. All hands fold themselves into prayer before it, all hands clasp themselves in reverence to it; there is nothing realer than it. It is the highest thing, higher even than violence; it is the highest violence.

When I became accustomed and the haze dissipated, I could see that inside that place was whiteness, similar to the ubiquitous whiteness in the hospital but not exactly the same. It wasn't fluorescent and glossy, it was matte and dull like the shell of an egg, a slight hint of yellow-green lurking underneath that made it nauseating, that made my eyes swim and dance with the threat of sickness. What would be there underneath the shell— if I scraped at the white, if I cracked it open, what could I find within? But I couldn't reach out and touch the white, because I couldn't locate the confines of the room at all, couldn't trace a wall or a ceiling or a horizon; when I looked out it was like the white went on and on forever in every direction. It overwhelmed my senses, making my mind stagger and give up on trying to orient itself. The only aspect of the place I could be certain about was that there was a floor, not only because my feet were planted firmly on it, but because I could see the person a short distance away from me sitting cross-legged on it. But I couldn't find any source of light that was enabling me to see this, to see my feet on the ground and my hands in front of me and the man sitting there; everything shone brightly but without a lamp, without a sun. It shone from some internal source, like the bioluminescence of a deep-sea creature; as though the whole place was a living organism, shining with its own sentient power. I knelt down and placed my hands against the floor, spreading the fingers out carefully, and it was hard and cool like marble. I lowered my body, rolling my legs in front of me and crossing them to mimic the man across from me, and stared at him without fear or even curiosity. I felt that I already knew him, better than perhaps anyone else.

The man sitting in front of me was emaciated, his ribs and collarbone jutting out of his skin, the bottom of his rib cage dramatic against the hollow of his gut; thin folds of skin drooped around his skeletal hands, thin folds of skin drooped around his tendon-and-vein-webbed neck. Long hair, dark, dull, and fragile, dropped from his head down his back, with strands falling across his chest and collecting in his lap. His legs, like his arms, were long and thin and insect-like, with frail feet folded underneath them. The dry, cracked lips on his face were slightly parted; his eyes were closed and lightly fluttering as though from a bad dream. His smooth, hairless face was slim and feminine, and nearly healthy-looking in comparison with the gauntness of his body, with bright, even skin. He was muttering something to himself quietly, in an endless stream, but no words came out; nothing I could hear. On the left side of his chest, between the nipple and the bottom of the rib cage, there was a hole, a narrow slit that was several inches wide. Its edges were smooth and even with the skin, not red and raw as though it were a wound or a scar; it was as though it were a natural feature of his body. Liquid was streaming out of the slit, a black, thick substance flowing evenly and unendingly down into his lap, splashing onto the floor and moving across it like a stream. I stood up from the floor easily, my body not aching or tired, and moved to follow the flow of the muck, the river that cut through the overbearing whiteness. My steps were careful as I walked along the side of the stream, the sound of my footsteps swallowed by the white floor, muffled so that I couldn't hear them at all, despite the hard, marble-like surface of the ground. But I could hear the thick trickling flow of the ooze, gurgling and frothing and bubbling, the eager, lively murmurings of liquid in motion. I followed it as it travelled across the ground, my body strong and light but my mind heavy and slow, like I was peacefully underwater. When I had walked for just a few minutes the stream suddenly ended; there was a circular gap in the ground, clean-cut and perfectly round like an ice-fishing

hole, around the size of my hand. The black, thick substance flowed straight down into it, all of it falling
through the hole, down into the depths. I crouched on
my hands and knees and, adjusting myself carefully so
that I could see around the falling stream, peered down
into the hole.

Through the hole was a brightness that was brighter
than the glow of the white room; I couldn't make out
anything at first because of this and blinked hard, squinting until the shock of the glare wore off. On the other
side of the hole the sun was shining with all of its strength;
glowing fiery and hot, bearing down with ferocity, with
severity, as though trying to ignite the flat landscape
beneath it. The ground underneath the terribly bright sun
was covered in weeds and grass, a mosaic of patches that
were scorched dead yellow and trembling or that were
lively green, and standing in the midst of these patches
was a horse, bending its long alien snout down over the
mess of vegetation. Its gentle, leathery snout with nostrils
like gaping caves carved in stone, nostrils carved into the
massive boulder of its head. Lining its sad eyes were whis-
kery, tender lashes, the large, dark pupils sitting behind
them like giant glimmering marbles, and suspended in the
pupils were gloom and melancholy, and hovering starkly,
frighteningly, behind the gloom and melancholy were
timidity and intelligence. The impossible mass of the animal's body was ancient and visceral, both a part of the

world and alien to it; the body wrapped in the slick oily brown-black of its coat, its hues shifting subtly as the horse moved. Behind the body its tail flicked fitfully against the air, and across the muscular neck was a line of flowing hair, dark and shining and human-like. Between the horse's torso and the ground its legs stood in the grass like weapons: bony, gnarled staffs encoded with the threat of their strength and virility, of their speed. The animal was beautiful in a terrible, sad way; completely innocent. I was looking out at it through a hole in a wall, looking horizontally across the landscape instead of down onto it through a hole in the sky, as I should have been. The dark substance was flowing out through the hole, around my eye, down the wall and across the landscape where it gurgled in the weeds, seeped into the soil, puddled in the dirt, staining the green and yellow and brown field with black oil. In the distance the horse stepped cautiously through the brush on its sturdy legs, lowering its neck and sniffing at the green parts, raising its head and gazing disaffectedly toward the horizon, not noticing me as I looked out at it, not noticing as the substance streamed through the hole.

I stood back up in the matte white space. My hands were dirty, stained with grime; I had gotten some of the substance on them and it was sticky and thick against my skin, clinging to me. I wiped my palms on the front of my pants, leaving large dark streaks, but my hands still

looked the same afterwards, as though the substance had
simply duplicated itself on contact with another surface,
as though whatever it touched could never be free of it,
would be stained for eternity. The man was still seated
with his legs crossed on the floor, his face bowed, his eyes
vacant and far-off, not focused on anything; there was
nothing in his face other than the smooth gleam of his
skin and the perfect snowblind silence. With the ooze
leaking out of his wound he was a fountain, quiet and
devout, committed to his task. I stepped away from the
hole in the ground and walked back toward him, and as I
walked toward him I could feel someone else doing the
same, from the opposite side of the room. I couldn't hear
their footsteps or see them but I could feel the slight shifts
in the atmosphere, a tingling awareness at the back of my
head that alerted me to another presence, a familiar,
intimate presence. I spun around looking for it, my heart
pounding in my throat, the blood whipping around in my
body; my blood that was happy to rush along the same
pathway, again and again for years, no exit, no way to get
off the ride, my blood that was resigned to its biology,
to the singularity of its purpose, and I wanted to be, too.
I wanted to be resigned to a singular grand purpose; with
all of my movements and thoughts I begged for it. The
man sat still with the ooze falling out of him and behind
him I could see the thing approaching, the shape of its

body vague against the luminescent white of the room, like it was emerging from a cloud, a splotch of colour marring the uniformity.

I was in front of the man with the fountain-body, looking over his shoulder at the thing approaching us. As it got closer its body clarified in the midst of the whiteness, as it approached us with even steps on its tiny legs, the tiny legs that carried its tiny body, a body that hadn't truly defined itself yet, hadn't yet laid claim to the form it was fated to take. When I saw it I could feel the emptiness inside me, the emptiness of my muscles tensing and relaxing, the emptiness of blood shifting back and forth, of the cyclical pulsing of organs. Nothing as solid as a voice, as the presence of another, of a thing greater than me, just the mechanical indifference of biology. It was completely gone, the blessing that had placed me outside of the confines of myself, the blessing that had freed me from my death and swaddled me warmly, that had grabbed me by the loose skin on the nape of my neck and placed me in an open field, taught me which direction to run in and how to run as quickly as I could. The blessing that had chosen me, that had turned the key in the lock and slid open the large metal doors, shown me what lay inside the hidden vault, the vault that had blended into the wall until it was pointed out to me. The blessing that had permitted me to understand the secret sickly sweetness hidden in the pit of each passing moment, and

I had lowered my trembling tongue to it and tasted it, lapped it up until it melted under the heat of my breath. It had left me and I was empty again, not knowing in which direction to run, not knowing how to continue on. The child walked out of the matte whiteness and stood beside the emaciated man, looking at me with strange, indifferent eyes.

The man finally raised his head and looked at me, with the same incomprehensible, vacant expression as the child's, an unbothered animal loosely considering its familiar scenery. I couldn't tell if there was intelligence behind his eyes, or something different, something I couldn't quite understand, a different way for a mind to engage with the world around it, not greater or less than intelligence but outside its scope entirely. The child had the same thing in its eyes; it was a cold, alienating gaze, and with both of their gazes locked on me they isolated me from them and from the white space. I was stabbed by the acute sense that I didn't belong there, that I was an intruder, that everything about me clashed grotesquely with the air: the contours of my clothes and flesh, my hair and my arms and legs, the way I breathed. I was a hideous accent against the serene atmosphere of the room, a drop of oil in a glass of water. My heart beat sluggishly against the wall of my chest, and now that my awareness had sharpened with anxiety I could feel, inside me, almost imperceptibly, the crawling of insects. Inside my body were dozens and dozens of little insects, enacting their drama in the gaps between my ribs, burrowing holes into the softer parts of my marrow, fighting and crawling and shedding exoskeletons inside me; I was the stage for the drama they were enacting. This whole time I had been the stage. And as I felt the insects crawl over me there was something else, something that was waiting patiently for me to understand it; that I was inching closer to understanding, but that I couldn't bear to understand, a burden I would never be able to bear.

The child held out its hand to me with the palm upturned, and the drama that the insects were in the midst of exploring stopped in its course. I stepped outside the way the narrative was unfurling and things slid into a different gear; the child's extended hand was another option. The man on the floor uncrossed and recrossed his spindly legs, turning his upper body to face the child, and with his left hand touched the tip of his thumb to the tip of his forefinger, the other three fingers extended out. With the two fingers pressed together he reached out and touched the child on the left side of its chest, just below the nipple. The man traced a line with his fingers a few inches long and then twisted his body back to face forward again, returning his hands to his lap and facing down. The child just stood there with the same blank expression, hand held out to me, waiting for me to clasp it with my own. On its chest where the man had traced his fingers the flesh began to part, without redness of blood or friction, opening up smoothly and gently as though tenderly unfurling a pair of wings after a long period of rest, and from behind the parting flesh the dark substance began to stream out; first hesitantly, in little drops, and then in earnest, flowing forth, falling over the child's body onto the floor. The substance flowed across the floor next to the stream that flowed from the man's body, the two streams twisting and curving parallel to one another until a few feet away they joined together in one singular thick, full river, before dropping off into the hole in the ground.

The whiteness of the room wrapped around me like a cocoon, and I stood quietly waiting to see what would happen, unsure of where to plant my next step, waiting for a guiding light to descend onto the top of my head and drape itself over my shoulders, over my back, over my stomach and calves, to warm my muscles and stimulate my feelings, propel me into motion, show me which way to go. The child stood patiently, hand held out to me, the dark substance streaming out of its body and over the floor, and even without words I knew what it was saying to me: *sit with us and work.* I could perform the work alongside them, and through the work I would keep all things at a safe distance from each other, I would keep myself at a safe distance from all other things. And as we worked, overtop of the world would hover an illusion weaved to keep the fantasy intact, to keep the world believing it's made of solid objects pressed together when it's really made out of gas, out of inexact sentiments and necessary delusions. I could become an artisan of the impenetrable distance between everything, I could become a tool for the dream of the desire to keep everything apart; I could blend into the throbbing eggshell-white of the room, melt into it like sugar under intense heat. If I became a tool here, my death couldn't scare me, I could hold my death in the palm of my hand, clenching and unclenching as I pleased. But I couldn't be instructed to join them; this was a choice I had to make on my own, of my own volition. I didn't move toward the child's out-stretched hand, I didn't step back. And through the hole in the floor the black substance fell, a terrible waterfall nourishing the world.

I emerged from the emptiness with a deep ache inside my body, the bed's hard plastic frame jutting through the thin mattress and pressing up against me, putting pressure on my sore hips, on my shoulders and my spine and my neck, but the hard plastic frame pushing up against me wasn't the cause of the real ache. The ache in me had roots, twisted and knotted and lengthy, burrowed so far inside me that I couldn't find the ends of them, stretching themselves out throughout my body; the ache went beyond tender points and muscular tension, it wasn't something that could be resolved by holding a stretch or by alternating heat, ice, heat, ice, heat. The pain was so intertwined with the body as to be inseparable from it, was no longer an occupant of the house but had melted into the walls, had become part of the beams that held up the structure. If I tried to separate myself from it my body would collapse; the ache was the body, the body was the ache. I slowly scooted up to a seated position and took stock of myself. My body looked much the same as before, and I could move it with relative ease: my feet could be rotated back and forth, my legs could lift off the bed and return back down, my arms could be stretched out and then returned to my sides, all my appendages were attuned to my commands. But my feet weren't sheathed in shoes or socks, and my pants and underwear were missing as well; instead of my clothes I was wrapped in an off-white gown, the garment reaching down to just below my knees and tied roughly around the waist by a ratty length of frayed string. I could feel the cool, stale air of the room on my skin, and when I reached under the thin fabric of the gown to feel my torso with my fingers they were cold, too, my body automatically recoiling from the freeze of my own touch. Just below the navel I felt something stuck to me, and when I brought my fingers to the area they found a thin rectangular strip stretching hip to hip; I clawed at it trying to tear it off but it was affixed very tightly to the skin. I tugged the gown further apart, writhing like a snake shedding its skin, and looked down at my lower abdomen; there was a large medical bandage adhered to me, a slight stain of dark red-brown underneath the white. Feverishly I picked at a corner of the bandage with my dirty, broken nails, trying to get under the adhesive and get a grip on it, and when finally a fingernail slipped under it I pulled hard, the skin stretching out uncomfortably with the bandage and then separating from it with a sharp, burning feeling. The underside of the gauze was dirtied with dry splotches of what looked like blood, but the flesh that it had covered was unblemished, only reddened from the irritation of yanking the bandage off. I balled it up and tossed it to the floor, then swung my legs over and touched my feet to the cold ground, standing up dizzily, blood scattering from my head down my torso and making the room blur and spin for a brief moment.

A tray had been placed next to the door on a pair of folding legs, my clothes neat on top of it. I walked over unsteadily and picked them up, and in my hands they were soft and fresh, imbued with the faint scent of dampness. Tucked tidily under the tray's legs were my shoes, the dirt and dust wiped from them. I untied the gown's ratty string and shrugged the garment off my shoulders so that it slipped off my body and landed in a sad puddle on the floor, and stepped carefully out of the puddle to mechanically pull on my underwear, pants, shirt, socks, shoes, my limbs snapping and flailing, my body stretching out and rolling back in, bending from the hips to twist the shoelaces, yanking them tight. To the side of the door the dark glass panel glimmered, its red laser eye gazing disinterestedly at me; I waved my hand in front of it, I pushed my palm against it, I lowered my face to it so that it could look at me, and nothing happened. The sliding door was open just a crack and I grasped the side of the door and pulled it the rest of the way open, letting the white light of the hallway run its fingers over the shadows of the tiny room. I put my feet through the doorway, cautiously, and then my legs and my torso, exiting the room and creeping tentatively, body aching and eyes darting over the white hallway: the white walls, white floor, white ceiling. I was looking for someone but no one was there to greet me, not with flowers or otherwise. I moved down the hallway slowly and it was like I was stuck swimming in a thick substance, pushing up against the weighted resistance as I moved, my feeble limbs flapping in tiny, difficult motions. My breaths moved slowly, too, each of my inhales spanning minutes, my exhales stretching out indefinitely. People in colourless starched uniforms moved up and down the corridor, their legs fluttering quickly against the hard white floor, blurs of motion as they rushed past me on their quiet shoes and their bouncing feet, and as they passed me I reached out to them, my hand up in the air, waving them down, their eyes briefly darting over to me and then straight back ahead, their movements never slowing and gait never changing and all their faces were the same face: white mask covering the mouth or pulled below the chin, hair tied back or cropped short, but beyond these slight variations they were all identical. I opened my mouth and shouted out at them, shouting through the pit of emptiness that was stuck in my chest, a single sharp syllable like a whistle. There was nothing else I could say, no words that I could form, and the interior of the sound was hollow and weightless, translucent, nearly crushed into nothingness by the dense air of the hallway the moment it brushed past my lips. One of the people walking past slowed momentarily to look me over and I looked him in his eye, behind his eye, to where I could see him rotating a thought in the inner workshop of his mind; then the thought stopped rotating and vanished and his hand came up, waving to me dismissively, his feet whirring into motion once more as he continued down the hallway.

As he propelled himself down the hall I stood there and waited for someone else to walk by, standing in the middle of the corridor with my arms hanging limply by my sides. A woman began to approach from the end of the hallway, moving at a high speed, her footsteps light against the cold white ground, and as she flew past me my hand shot out like a grappling hook, my claw-fingers around her arm, my sharp eyes drilling into her face. She stopped and spun to face me, and stretched over her face was a cheap mask of smiling politeness, a tensely upturned mouth and the thin curves of her eyebrows, all above the neat white layers of her uniform. I opened my mouth to try to push my questions out but she interrupted me before I could, her speech all rushing quickly like a rapid river, frothing and chaotic, her words stumbling and falling over each other in their race to exit her mouth, trampling over each other like they were escaping a burning theatre; *hello, do you need something, are you looking for someone, I'm busy right now but I will . . .* She cut herself off quickly, a sudden unsignalled merge on a gridlocked highway, her eyebrows raising slightly, quivering on her forehead: *oh, you're room 171?* I turned and looked back the way I had come, squinting toward the doorway of the tiny room, looking for some confirmation. She continued on without waiting: *what a lively child you had, so eager.* The words hit me burning-hot, scalding me, my heart quickening, fingers tensing tighter around her arm as her smile deepened until it stretched out her face, her flesh pushed up over her cheeks, delicate wrinkles carved out around her brightening eyes. *So strong-willed, the whole team was just in love, what a cute face too!* I tried to speak but all that moved through my throat was ragged breathing and a low hum of unrefined sound, my mouth wouldn't sculpt out the words, my tongue thick and heavy and useless against the palate. *Just look at this, look at what it did to my hand*, shakes of laughter spinning out of her face as she raised the hand to show me, holding it before my face so that I could see that the nails were all gone, the fleshy tips of the fingers raw and red, the skin peeling and wrinkled. The laughter crackled out of her deep smile like burning embers jumping off a campfire, *it pulled them right out, every single one, can you believe it, that's something you don't see every day.* I let go of her arm, my hand dropping to my side; I didn't understand, and the building pulsed and glowed around me in my dumbstruck silence until finally I was able to speak, until finally words dropped out of my dry lips and I asked her where the child had gone. The smile fell from the nurse's face and she shrugged weakly, half-heartedly, her gaze sliding off my face as she looked down the hall, in the direction she had been rushing toward. Without looking back at me she began to walk again, quickly, her feet tapping quietly against the cool white floor, her white uniform billowing around her as she rounded the corner and disappeared.

I was left alone with the emptiness inside of my chest, left to haunt the hallway while the institution churned and belched around me. The hall was like a conveyer belt moving an endless stream of bodies across the floor, all of them with the same face, all of them with bleached and starched uniforms, all of them unboundedly productive and focused, mannequins pulsing with jittery energy; and enveloping everything was the pulsing white of the building, fluorescent and piercingly bright. The whole enterprise was a seamless mechanical process that ignored me, that excluded me, that had nothing to do with me, flowing around me with insurmountable indifference. Tiny and insignificant before the mountainous reality of the building, I had nothing to cling to. My understanding had been completely lost, had been shaved roughly off me like a layer of dry skin under a pumice stone, and after losing my understanding I was continuing to lose mass, to shrink and shrink, and I would continue to shrink until I was so withered and feeble that I would disappear into the environment around me—the building would bend itself around me like a great wet mouth and swallow without chewing, encase me in the walls and under the cold white floor, digest me until I ended up as nothing but a memory floating in the midst of the institution's processes; and this swallowing and digestion wouldn't even be targeted, it would just be a matter of course. There was nothing I could use to determine the boundaries of myself, no utensil I could wield to trace out my form—to sketch out my head, shoulders, hips, knees, heart, name, will. I wouldn't know what to draw. I needed to place myself within some sort of border, something with a substantial reality to it, a box I could climb into, a new form of understanding that I could tether myself to, and I wouldn't find it in the great glossy white institution; I had to get out.

Slowly I inched through the hallway, remaining close to the wall, the cool solidity of it under my hand steadying me, reassuring me that the biome I was trapped in was made up of physical aspects—that I could, if I wanted, slam my fist through the wall, tear the synthetic fibres away and climb out of the hole. With my hand against the wall I moved through the building, squeezing myself carefully, painfully, through the arteries of the great machine. My steps trembled along the hallway, trembled around a corner, my insides spinning around and around, all my organs and thoughts and feelings replaced only by an ancient nauseating carousel that creaked and shrieked and never ceased to spin, its cracked wood and rusted metal bending under the pressure of its endless spinning. I turned another corner, guided by nothing except the dizzy fever that twisted hotly under my skin, understanding nothing, not even truly able to understand the deficit of my understanding, just try-ing to get out. Somehow, on the way out, the entire institution had become an impossible labyrinth without changing its layout at all. Everything was ostensibly the same, I vaguely remembered being pushed through these same hallways on my way in, but it had become maze-like. The building had overlaid its architecture on the labyrinth of my own mind, so that as I walked through its hallways I navigated my insides as well: a square of floor was a memory of a field, a segment of wall was the sound of my name, a corner was a feeling that dwelled inside me, deep inside me, flickering like a lantern in the dark. I couldn't find how I fit into this lab-yrinth of myself, didn't know what contortions I was supposed to make to be able to resonate with it, so that I could take control of it. And because of this I couldn't navigate the building either, because of the way that it laid itself over my mind like a sketch on translucent paper placed over another sheet.

After turning corner after corner and becoming adrift in the snowblindness of the white hallways, I finally found, cut into the bleached skeleton of the hospital, a shaded nook: a little cubby off to the side, a secret inner pocket within the endlessly unfurling white walls. As I haunted closer toward it I saw the squat chairs, offensively simple pieces of curved plastic, scratched and tinted from use, yellowed and greyed with black peeking out from under the thin scratches. A row of these chairs was affixed loosely along an aluminum bar just above the ground, the whole row squeaking and rocking as the person seated at the end adjusted their body, uncrossing and recrossing their legs. There was a low acrylic table in front of the row of chairs, a single piece of transparent material that was bent downwards at both ends so that the tabletop was also the legs; among the fingerprint smudges that covered its surface was a messy pile of magazines, glossy and colourful. The person sitting at the end of the row leaned over and fingered the magazine on the top of the pile, flicking through the pages quickly, barely looking at it. When I stood right before the waiting nook looking at them, they glanced up at me, and I saw their face and recognized them, and they stood up immediately but unhurriedly, pulling themselves up to their full height, their long legs on heeled black boots. They walked over to me without a word, their arm extending out and looping around my back, pushing me gently but firmly, making me walk quickly down the hall alongside them. I was trying to say something, something I couldn't yet understand, and the labour of looking for what I needed to say with the swollen, useless muscles of my tongue and my jaw soon became too tiring; I closed my mouth, closing myself off to language. We approached the front entrance, where the woman was still standing behind the desk, nearly motionless, frozen within the white of the floor and walls and ceiling. Her head didn't move as we passed her, as we drifted toward the sliding glass doors and then through the doors, ejected out into the open air. The car was still sitting there at the front, quiet and cold with its dark, opaque windows. The driver let go of me and strode over to the car in long strides, opening the passenger door and motioning for me to get in. How could I possibly move to the car, lower my body onto the leather seat, reach over and pull the belt over my body, place my feet on the floor mat? I wasn't even there, all that was there was the lingering afterthought, an afterimage maintained by an environment that hadn't yet come around to acknowledging my absence. When I stretched my hands out in front of me I could see the edges of them evaporating into the air around them, aerosol particles of skin and flesh floating off, nearly imperceptible. If I managed to get into the car I would disintegrate into the air vents, disperse out the crack of the window, vanish through the exhaust pipe in a final belch of dark, pungent smoke.

The driver stared at me with large unblinking eyes, face blank like a lizard sunning itself on a stone, face blank like the smooth surface of a plastic table. They stood by the open passenger door, one hand on the outer handle, the other hand frozen in mid-air gesturing toward the car's interior, observing me, their eyes penetrating mine. It was as though thin needles were extending from the dark depths of their pupils and stretching across the air toward my eyes, piercing my pupils, prodding around in the deep insides of my eyes where I lived, trying to locate me. The driver's mouth moved slowly, saying something to me, wrapping its lips around each word and ejecting it out, but I couldn't hear what they were saying because inside me all there was was the spinning feverish carousel, creaking and whipping around. They swept their arm to gesture to the passenger seat and nodded at me, and there was nowhere else for me to go, and I stepped forward slowly, feet plodding across the ground, and ducked into the car, leaning back into the leather seat. The driver clicked the door shut after me and walked around the car. I listened and couldn't hear anything except the muffled ambience of the world outside the vehicle; I turned around slowly and behind me there was nothing other than the empty back seat, the rear windshield behind it. The other door opened and the driver lowered their body onto the seat and plunged the key into the ignition with their long, thin fingers, and the car erupted into violence. They swerved out from under the hospital entrance's canopy and down the road, and as we rolled down the winding driveway the building got smaller and smaller in the rear-view mirror. My vision blurring from fatigue and frailty, I let the landscape out the window be eroded into a mosaic of soft, indefinite colours, gave up on attempting to focus, let the buildings fold into each other, let the road blend into the curb and the sidewalk, let the boundaries of everything disintegrate. The understanding and purpose I had been briefly given had been taken from me definitively, and without its shield I was naked, decaying; I trembled in the passenger seat, skin turning grey, finger-nails brittle and cracking.

The sunlight bounced off the windows of the buildings we sped past and I squinted as it hit my eyes; the driver yanked the shift stick to change gears, their foot pushing steadily against the pedal, the car humming louder. I leaned back in my seat, sinking into its plush comfort, floating on the sickly cloud of my fatigue, the sweet earthy smell of the leather in my head, and in the moment before I fell into sleep I caught myself and pulled myself back because I had seen it. In the moment where I was falling backward into sleep, from within the sudden rush of ver-tigo, within the feeling of falling from a great height, I had opened a secret eye and seen it: it was everywhere. It was hidden between the dashboard and the space under it; it was squeezed between the glass of the windshield and the road beyond it; squeezed between the sheets of glass. It was in my body, too, between the layers of skin, between the chambers of my heart, between the cells of blood as they rushed through my arteries and veins. I could find it again, that special hidden place that was everywhere, that was in between all things, pushing up against the boundaries of everything, keeping everything apart. I could see it, with my secret eye I could see it, and I knew that through it I could understand; I just had to reach for it and it would wrap itself around me, wrap me in white armour, wrap me in its language, give me a shield that would stop me from disintegrating. All I had to do was reach for it; it was *I* who had to decide, *I* who had to make the first move that would throw the sequence into motion.

We drove on in silence and I watched the sun lowering itself carefully onto the passing landscape, slowly moving toward the horizon, still far from it; the day was not yet over. The town was distant in the rear windshield, the earth around us once again flat, stretching itself lazily out for miles and miles, the landscape a palette of simple colours: yellow, brown, green, and in the sky, blue, azure, white, a vision painted by a child, by an elderly man filling the boredom of retirement with a canvas. In my frail, exhausted condition time moved around me rather than with me; my mind couldn't move quickly enough to keep up with it, so I relaxed and let it rush by me. The events sequenced themselves around me, irrelevant to me. But shortly I would have to make a decision, shortly I would have to choose the shape of what came next.

The car had stopped at some point without me noticing; it was stalling in place with its engine purring and coughing inside its casing. I turned and the driver was looking at me, their pupils dark and huge against the shining pearly white of the sclera. Looking into their eyes made everything around them blur and twist and spin, hallucinatory and nauseating, as though I had ingested something psychoactive, my face quickly becoming flushed and sweaty. They reached slowly toward me, stretching their long fingers out, and pulled open the plastic door of the glovebox, which clicked and swung down; I reached into it and felt around, wrapping my hand around the single item that was inside, bulky and long, soft under my careful fingertips. I pulled the object out of the glovebox into the light, into my lap, and studied it: a leather sheath, dark brown leather with even stitching around the edges, as long as my forearm and a bit heavy, the handle of the knife jutting out from the bottom of the sheath. The handle was the colour of dull gold and curved like a crescent moon. It was carved with tiny symbols: a sun, a star, a moon, the head of a lion on a serpentine body, a man with the head of a bull wearing a crown. I slid the dagger out from its sleeve and the blade was sleek, shining richly like a precious jewel, the sunlight glinting off it, the edge tapered expertly thin, sharp and beautiful. My fingers were prudent and light before the force of its presence, the danger of its presence.

I slid the sharp blade back into the sheath and looked up to see the driver still staring at me with their vortex eyes, burning eyes; they nodded slowly and lifted themselves out of their seat, bending their body over me, and yanked my door open, shoving it outward. A breeze shyly entered the car and tussled my hair, bringing with it the smell of open air, sky, dirt, animal life. When I smelled it and felt the wind it was like I had been there a hundred times before, like I had always been there, pulling my body up from the seat of the car while the breeze washed over me; and I was overwhelmed with fatigue from the sudden conviction that I had been sentenced to repeat this movement over and over without end, forever, until time and space finally peeled themselves apart and put a stop to everything. My legs nearly buckled from the wave of hopelessness that zipped through me like a bolt of electricity through a copper wire, but I steeled myself before I fully collapsed to the asphalt of the road, one hand grabbing the door and the other holding the sheathed knife. The driver sat back in their seat watching me, saying nothing as I stood up and left the car, closing the door.

When the door crunched shut the engine's purring became more earnest, urgent, the rubber tires spinning hotly against the road, throwing up dust as the car turned around and sped off back in the direction it had come from, fast like the weapon that it was. I was left standing on the side of the road, watching as the vehicle became smaller and smaller, watching until my eyes couldn't follow it any longer, until it disappeared into the horizon. There was a feral ache in my head that stretched down into my neck and shoulders, a pulsing beat like a logger rhythmically sending his axe into a tree. A river of pain flowing through my body; no, it was that my body was detritus floating through an ocean of pain, the water lapping at me, pulling me into it as I slowly fell apart and became part of the ocean, little pieces of me swallowed by schools of fish, little pieces of me eroding into nothingness in the salty water. There was nothing that differentiated my body from what happened to it; there was nothing that differentiated me from what happened to me. I turned away from the road and looked at the scene I had been pulled into: in the near distance was the field, and within the field was a barn; next to the barn wall was the horse, dipping its neck into the tall messy weeds, the hair on its neck rustling in the wind, the sun shining majestically onto the brown-black of its coat.

When I looked at the horse standing there in the field, suddenly there was nothing else; suddenly there was nothing before the moment when my eyes alighted upon the animal. When I looked at it I was thrust into the shock of the unending present, and the present was a raw and jagged edge, like being thrown directly into deep waters before learning how to swim in the shallows; flailing and splashing, lungs burning with grief, with desperation. When I looked at the horse I became myself, and whatever came before was torn to shreds, ripped apart by the scraping, splitting hook that was my eyes alighting upon the horse. I stepped away from the asphalt into the grass and weeds, moving toward the barn, toward the horse, and the animal didn't lift its head to me as I began to approach it; it stayed frozen where it was, its tail flicking indifferently at the air. When I got closer to the barn I saw the hole in the wall, saw the black gunk flowing through it, the thick tar pouring out as though from an endless fountain. I saw the substance seeping into the soil, muddying the yellow-green weeds. It pooled around my feet, sloshing, gurgling, squelching as I plodded through it. And in the barn wall I could also see the cracks, could also see the way that the cracks housed hundreds and hundreds of timid bugs, their little mouths chewing and little legs scrabbling at the rotten and decaying wood; the insects that were creeping and

crawling, fighting and gorging, fucking and dying on
the stage of the scene I was taking part in, on the stage
of the scene I had been cast for. Overhead the light bulb
pulsed yellow and hot, swinging slowly back and forth,
cruelly illuminating the scene where I was bound to the
chair. No, no—overhead it was the sun that pulsed yellow
and hot, swinging itself slowly to the horizon, cruelly
illuminating the scene where I walked through the field
to the horse, its mournful face not turned to me. My shoes
were covered in the sticky, pitch-black gunk, making my
legs heavy as I moved through the field, each step a massive, impossible effort, but I was so close to the horse I
could almost touch it, I could nearly reach my hand out
and caress its soft coat. From overhead, the light cast
shadows down over the man's face. No, no, that's not
it—from overhead, the light cast shadows down over the
head of the horse; and someone's tired fingers were
around the handle of the blade. The knife was in someone's hand. My fingers were around the knife's intricate
handle, feeling the detail of the carvings, pulling the
blade out of its leather sheath and letting the sheath fall
to the ground. The blade was sharp and glimmering in
the sun, and in my head was the man's ragged breath, the
dribble of his spit and the croak of his language, and in
my head were the insects swarming over the walls, chewing at the mortar in between the stones, and in my head

was the pain as the rope was tightened around my wrists. All that awful noise pounding against me and drilling into my bones, tearing me apart, razing the landscape of my body. And then everything fell silent; and then everything was quiet and still. And then there was just the soft rustle of the breeze against the field and the small sound of the horse's breath through its snout, and it was all quiet because I understood. I understood, and I knew what I had to do next.

Thank you to all the friends who read early drafts and offered feedback and encouragement. Thank you to my editor Haley Cullingham, and everyone else at Strange Light/Penguin Random House Canada, for believing in this book and helping to get it into the world. Thank you to my life partner, Ziya, without whose support, love, and companionship this book would not have been possible.

Nour Abi-Nakhoul is a writer and editor from Toronto, currently based in Montreal. Her writing has appeared in a variety of Canadian and American publications.